HARMONY

Visit us at www.boldstrokesbooks.com

HARMONY

by
Karis Walsh

2011

HARMONY

ISBN 10: 1-60282-237-9
ISBN 13: 978-1-60282-237-5

This Trade Paperback Original Is Published By
Bold Strokes Books, Inc.
P.O. Box 249
Valley Falls, NY 12185

First Edition: August 2011

CREDITS
Editor: Ruth Sternglantz
Production Design: Susan Ramundo
Cover Design By Sheri (graphicartist2020@hotmail.com)

Acknowledgments

Thank you to…

My family, for wholeheartedly supporting every dream I choose to pursue.

Radclyffe, for turning away from her own beautiful writing long enough to make a difference in LGBTQ publishing in general, and this writer's life in particular.

Sheri, for creating such a gorgeous cover, and the "behind the pages" BSB staff, for tirelessly working to produce such quality products.

And my editor, Ruth Sternglantz, for sharing her insight and knowledge as she helped me turn a scruffy manuscript into a book. I had fun and learned a lot—can it get any better than that?

Dedication

For Mom
With love

CHAPTER ONE

Andy Taylor hurried through the well-dressed crowd in the church foyer, carefully keeping her viola case from knocking into anyone's legs, more concerned about jostling her instrument than snagging nylons or bruising shins. The number of people she had to avoid meant she wasn't as late as she had feared, and she sighed with relief when she finally made it through the gauntlet to the door that led into the sanctuary. She pushed through the swinging door and made her way quickly up the outside aisle toward the rest of her quartet.

"You're late," Tina said, propping her violin between her legs and reaching for Andy's music.

"No shit," Andy whispered. The wedding party clustered around the altar, forming and reforming groupings for pictures like a well-trained school of fish. She breathed a silent prayer of gratitude that the photographer had delayed the start of the ceremony. She handed her viola to Richard to tune while she tightened the horsehair on her bow and slid a cake of rosin across its surface. He returned the instrument as Tina plopped her music, arranged in the proper order for today's ceremony, on her stand.

"Late night?" David asked with a wicked grin, his arm draped across his cello as he watched the silent performance of his three partners. "Did Her Highness need an ego boost before tonight's concert?"

"Her ego needs several boosts a night," Tina said with a frown. "So Lyssa wakes up on top of the world, and we're stuck with a worn-out shell of a violist."

Andy glared at her friends. Richard, as usual, didn't add any comments about her sometimes lover, but from the expression on his face it was clear he agreed with the assessment of the other two. Lyssa Carlyle, Andy's colleague in the Seattle Symphony, always managed to fall to pieces when she had a violin solo in a big concert. She would arrive on Andy's doorstep, weepy and practically begging for attention, and Andy let her in every time. After a night of flattery and exhausting sex, Lyssa would leave with a smile, ready to win the adulation of her audience. She was blissfully unconcerned with Andy's own performance schedule, needs, or satisfaction. And Andy was well aware that *after* Lyssa's concerts she would celebrate with one of her adoring fans, not with Andy. She and Lyssa would have to find a better compromise if their relationship could have any sort of future, but for now it was easier—and more predictable—just to play along as expected. Deep inside she knew the quartet was right and she was acting like a doormat, but she would never admit it out loud.

She bit back a rude retort about minding their own business when she saw the bride making her way over to them, walking sideways so her skirt would fit between pews. Andy assumed there must be a white dress somewhere under all of those rhinestones, and she hoped the petite brunette wouldn't collapse under the sheer weight of it during the ceremony.

"Thank goodness you're here," she said to Andy. "I was so worried when I only saw three musicians." Andy smiled tightly at the bride even as she silently chastised herself. She had almost been late for the gig, and Lyssa's ego was no excuse for spoiling someone's wedding day.

"Now, I hate to be a Bridezilla, but I have one little request," the girl continued, seemingly oblivious to the reaction that reference provoked from the musicians. Andy silently damned the show that made it seem cool to be obnoxious. They should be allowed to raise their fee every time that word was mentioned.

"It's your day," Andy jumped in, not trusting the other members of the group to answer politely.

"I would prefer that the help not socialize with the guests. I hope you don't mind?"

"Not at all," Andy answered truthfully, wondering if anyone could really think they took these gigs just so they could chat up someone's Aunt Martha and Uncle Pete after the ceremony.

"Good. Now we'll be seating the guests soon, so you can start playing anytime," the bride said before heading back to the photographer.

"The *help*?" Richard sputtered.

Andy tried not to laugh at his indignant expression. He was accustomed to a little more respect as a professor at a prestigious private college. "Don't worry," she said, patting his arm. "I know where she works. The next time I'm at the Gap, I'll leave a whole shitload of clothes in the dressing room for her to put away."

David played a bit of "God Save the Queen" pianissimo, and Andy glared at him before pasting on a smile as the bride returned.

"One more thing. I hope you won't mind leaving through the back exit after the ceremony."

"Of course not," Andy assured her. She stood up and helped the bride tug her dress free when it snagged on the pew's upholstery. A rhinestone dropped on the floor, and Andy quickly kicked it out of sight since she knew from experience even something so tiny could upset the delicate balance of a wedding day. Her first priority was to keep the bride calm. She would worry about her quartet's wounded pride later when she ushered them out the back way.

"Damn," Tina muttered as the bride slithered back between the pews. "I was hoping to get to know that tall bridesmaid. She ought to be all too willing to get out of that hideous dress."

❖

In spite of the pre-wedding drama, the ceremony itself went smoothly. Andy relaxed as she and her viola provided a measured harmony to the traditional wedding melodies. Even the stress of dealing with brides and grooms as they planned these involved affairs was worth it for these few minutes of peace and beauty. Andy was under no illusion that the marriages themselves would hold on to those attributes, but for a short time everyone could smile at one another and believe in true love. When she was a kid, Andy used to console herself during her parents' routine fights by picturing them on their wedding day. She figured they must have been in love at that moment, and she would try to force them back to happiness using only her youthful imagination. It had never worked, of course, but she still enjoyed being a part of the first moments of a marriage when everyone was still full of hope.

When the time came, the quartet did try to leave by the back door, but apparently the bride hadn't noticed the alarm system and emergency exit signs. Andy decided it would be better to risk the bride's wrath by mingling with her guests than to cause a panic by setting off the alarm, so she tried to keep the group moving quickly as they pushed their way through the crowd. Richard set off with purpose, but David seemed intent on breaking the bride's first rule by chatting with anyone who made the briefest eye contact with him, and Tina rubbernecked as she searched for her chosen bridesmaid.

"Beautiful ceremony, wasn't it?" David asked random people as Andy herded him along, trying in vain to spot Tina who had disappeared at the top of the steps. "Are you a friend of the bride? Wasn't she a vision?"

Andy grabbed his arm and pulled him toward the parking lot as Tina reappeared by her side, waving a small slip of paper.

"Too bad we're not playing at the reception," she said with a wicked smile. "I'll bet I could have gotten more than her phone number after a few glasses of champagne."

Andy shook her head at her unrepentant friend. Tina didn't need to moonlight as a musician since she made a good salary as a graphic designer, and Andy was certain she only took these wedding gigs to increase her dating pool, not her bank account. With her glossy brown hair and perfect body she managed to make out quite well—literally, all too often. "You guys are impossible. Is it too much to ask that we keep them happy for one hour so they'll recommend us to the next in line to get married?"

"We've got plenty of bookings as it is, and it's nearing the end of wedding season," Richard said as they met up with him at his van. He handed Andy a pile of manila folders. "Thank God you get to meet with these damned women in person since you're so intent on pleasing them."

She groaned and shifted her viola case so she could better balance the stack of paperwork. Richard managed the group's website and juggled their potential bookings with their individual schedules. But as soon as a date was set and any personal contact was required for planning, the brides became Andy's responsibility. "Why is this my job again?"

"Honestly? You're the only one who cares enough to put up with them. You're great at it, and you're going to love October Fifth." He tapped the top folder.

They were in the habit of referring to the brides by wedding date instead of name. "October Fifth, check," Andy said, peering in the slim folder. "A real bitch, I take it, since you're so thrilled to pawn her off on me?"

"No," Richard said with a slight frown. "She's more of the distracted-bride type. It's a last-minute booking, and she didn't know what music to pick or how many songs we should play. Flaky. Hopefully she'll have the wedding program set by the time you meet, but you might need to be more firm this time and get her to make some decisions."

"Firm?" Tina asked, sliding the folder from Andy's grasp. "I'll be glad to meet with this one."

Andy snatched October Fifth away from the grinning Tina. "He didn't mean whips-and-chains firm," she said. "I can handle it. No problem."

CHAPTER TWO

Two days later, Andy stood in the doorway of a downtown coffee shop during the lunchtime rush and scanned the room for October Fifth. She usually got a little tense before these bridal consultations since she never knew what to expect. Most of the brides were fun and easy to work with, but there was occasionally one who made her want to quit this business for good. A lesbian who still couldn't legally marry in most of the United States—including her home state of Washington—didn't seem to be the obvious choice when it came to helping people plan any part of a wedding, but Richard was right when he said she was the best one for the job. And he had been right about October Fifth. Most brides had requests for favorite songs or music from recent movies and at least a tentative schedule for the ceremony listed in the files that Richard compiled. This bride seemed to know very little beyond the date of her wedding. Even on the phone, she had seemed distant and vague when Andy called to set up this meeting. Andy had been the one to suggest this spot since it was close to the law firm where the bride worked as a paralegal.

Although she didn't have a physical description of October Fifth, other than her age of twenty-two, Andy quickly spotted her in the busy coffee shop. Except for a guy focused on his laptop, she was the only person who was sitting alone. She wasn't watching the doorway, like people waiting for a stranger usually are, but was instead staring out the window. Andy caught her breath as she looked across the room at the unmoving woman, only breaking her stare when someone jostled her from behind. She went to the counter and ordered a soy latte so she could collect herself for a moment before she met the bride. She had expected a ditzy young girl, but this woman looked older than the age listed in her file. Even seated, Andy could tell she was tall, and she wore a snugly fitted navy suit that hinted at full breasts and long legs. A plain rubber band held her hair, just that honey shade that edged away from brown and toward blond, in a high ponytail. Her appearance disconcerted Andy for some reason, since something about her seemed out of place. Maybe because she was an oasis of calm in the midst of a room full of chatting couples and groups, or because she lacked the expression of excited tension that Andy expected on a bride only days before her wedding.

It was definitely *not* because Andy felt any sense of attraction to her, or any curiosity about what was under that conservative blue suit.

Andy grabbed her drink and made her way over to October Fifth's table. She remembered Tina's grin when Richard told her to be firm with this one, and she nearly dropped her latte. "Jesus," she murmured as she shook herself mentally. Maybe this bride would have been safer with Tina.

"Brooke Stanton?" she asked as she approached the table, reminding herself in time not to actually call the woman October Fifth to her face.

Light blue eyes met Andy's like laser beams, and she had to reach out and use the back of a chair to steady herself. Brooke's gaze was blank for a moment as she simply stared at Andy.

"I'm Andrea Taylor," Andy continued, unsure now if she had found her client or had instead let her desire to talk to the beautiful woman lead her to the wrong conclusion. She felt a short-lived flash of hope that this really wasn't the straight soon-to-be Mrs. Foster. "My quartet is playing at your wedding?"

Brooke finally blinked and seemed to refocus her attention. "Yes, I'm Brooke. Sorry," she added with a humorless laugh, "you caught me daydreaming."

Andy pulled out the chair she had been gripping and sat down. "Perfectly natural," she said, keeping her tone light. "You must have a lot on your mind with the wedding and all…"

Brooke nodded vaguely and looked around the room as if noticing her surroundings for the first time. "How did you know who I was?"

Andy gestured at the binder on the table in front of Brooke. It was thick and white with cutout flowers and lacy hearts glued to the front cover. "Typical bridal accessory," she said.

"Jake's little sister made this for me," she said, giving it an awkward pat that pushed it across the table slightly. "Luckily she filled it with checklists and pictures or I wouldn't have known where to start."

"I'm sure there's a lot that goes into planning an event like this," Andy said, pulling out her own notebook that contained music and sample programs and setting it on the table next to Brooke's more ornate binder. "At least I can help make this part of it easier for you."

Andy was trying to slip into the persona of professional musician that she used with her more emotionally challenged brides, but Brooke leaned across the table and caught her off guard with those crystal eyes.

"Are you married, Andrea?"

"No. And most people call me Andy," she added, remembering too late that the point of using her full name was to maintain a professional distance.

"Not married?" Brooke asked. Her expression remained neutral, and Andy found herself curious about Brooke's assessment of her. "You must be dating? Serious boyfriend?"

"I have a girlfriend," Andy said, and then amended her statement. "Sort of."

"So you're a—"

"Right now I'm just a viola player," Andy said as she tapped the form in front of her with a pencil so she could shift the conversation off her life and back to music. She was unsure why she had shared any personal information with a woman she had just met. A client no less, and a straight woman who was about to be married.

Brooke blushed, and Andy hurried them past the awkward moment like she did whenever her meetings with brides encountered an emotional trigger. These were usually due to backfiring plans or meddling family members, and Andy was always the one to soothe the bride, not cause the stress in the first place. "Do you have any particular music in mind for the ceremony?"

Brooke shrugged. "You played at my cousin's wedding, and I remember liking your quartet. I guess you could play the same music. Her name was Lisa Stanton."

The name meant nothing to Andy, of course. Unless the bride or groom was a personal friend, or someone threw up or fainted during the ceremony, the quartet's past wedding gigs all blended into a sea of white dresses, tuxedoes, and faceless audiences. This didn't seem like an appropriate image to share with Brooke, so Andy simply pulled out the standard repertoire.

"Lisa Stanton, of course," she said smoothly. "I believe we played Pachelbel's "Canon in D" during the seating of the families and Bach's "Jesu, Joy of Man's Desiring" for the wedding party processional. Then it's Wagner's "Bridal Chorus" from *Lohengrin* when you walk down the aisle. That's the 'Here Comes the Bride' song," Andy added.

"Big, fat and wide," Brooke finished with a wince. "Great. And I'm still hoping to lose a few pounds before the wedding."

"Why would you want to do that?" Andy asked without thinking, never understanding why women who looked as healthy and beautiful as this one felt the need to diet. Brooke blinked at her in surprise, her eyes darkening slightly to a beautiful sky blue. "I mean, I think you look fine just as you are," Andy stammered, gesturing vaguely in Brooke's direction. She decided it was time to wrap up this meeting before she said anything else that could be misinterpreted as a pick-up line. "We played "Ave Maria" during the candle lighting and Beethoven's "Ode to Joy" for the recessional."

Brooke laughed suddenly, her distant expression transformed. "Do you really remember Lisa's wedding, or are those the songs you want me to choose?"

"They're pretty common choices," Andy admitted evasively, captivated by Brooke's smile and giving her one in return. "We'll be glad to make any changes you want or add music that has personal meaning for the two of you."

Brooke waved her hand in dismissal, a small smile still playing over her features. "What you said sounds just fine. I don't remember her wedding either. Can you write this down for me so I can take it to the printer's?"

Andy carefully copied the playlist, complete with composers and the full names of the quartet members, onto the form that Brooke removed from her massive binder. She added her nickname and phone numbers to the bottom of the page and handed it to Brooke.

"Call me if you want to add or change any of the songs," she said, pointing to her numbers. "We usually rehearse on Thursdays, so it'd be easiest if you let me know before that. Otherwise we'll see you next Friday."

"All right," Brooke said as she handed Andy a check that was double their normal fee for a wedding. Andy knew the other quartet members would want her to accept it without argument, but she felt uncomfortable taking advantage of Brooke.

"We usually play only at the ceremony and not the rehearsal," she said. "We've been in your church before, and we know where to set up, so you really don't need to book us for both days."

Brooke waved her hand at the check Andy tried to return. "Keep it. My mom wants to do a full run-through of the ceremony so she can be sure of timing and can coordinate it with the caterer."

Andy shrugged and tucked the check in her notebook. It wasn't her place to argue with the bride's wedding plans or to wonder why Brooke's voice sounded so resigned and weary. She resisted the urge to continue their conversation, maybe to coax another smile from her. Instead, she gave Brooke a receipt, and they stood and shook hands. With her heels on, Brooke met Andy's five-foot-nine height.

Andy did her best to keep her gaze from sliding down Brooke's long legs before she turned away, but as she left she was conscious of Brooke's gaze following her across the room.

❖

Brooke caught her lower lip between her teeth, forcing herself not to call Andy back to the table. She had barely registered her presence at first, seeing her as just another in a long line of faceless vendors connected to this wedding. She had been startled when her casual questioning had led her to find out that Andy was a lesbian, as if their simple conversation would reveal her own past.

She shook her head slightly. For a moment she had been tempted to try to flirt, maybe even to proposition, just for one last chance at the kind of sex she had only dreamed about. But that moment had passed, and Brooke knew she couldn't risk opening herself up to another woman and facing the pain that would follow. She was confident that after years of practice at hiding her true feelings, she hadn't let even one slip of dialogue or expression hint at them.

Her only moment of weakness had come when she refused Andy's offer to have the quartet play just at the ceremony. It had been her mother's idea to book them for the rehearsal as well, but Brooke knew she could have easily changed her mom's mind. She allowed herself the selfish desire to see Andy again on Friday, maybe to have one more chance to talk to her before their worlds inevitably separated.

What a shame too, she thought with a sigh as she opened her garish binder and added the quartet's program to the section marked "Music, Ceremony." Andy definitely looked like she could give Brooke a night that could fuel her fantasies for the next few decades of marriage. She was gorgeous with her short dark hair and those gold-flecked hazel eyes that had gazed at her with all of the seriousness of an anthropologist studying a bride-to-be in her native habitat. And her full lips looked so soft Brooke had nearly reached across the table to touch them when Andy smiled. But it was her hands that had most captivated Brooke's imagination. Slender and expressive, with short but neat nails, they had moved with such grace and strength that Brooke would have guessed her to be some sort of artist even if she hadn't known that she was a musician. Hands that she could imagine moving over her...

Brooke shut her binder with a snap and stood up. Hands that would never touch her that way. Because they belonged to a woman, and she belonged to Jake.

Chapter Three

A ndy slammed the phone down and started to pace back and forth in her apartment. What had she expected from Lyssa, anyway, she asked herself as she stalked from room to room, picking up random objects and banging them back in place. She ended up in the spare room that was filled with shelves of music and her instruments, hoping for that sense of peace and belonging that usually found her there, but feeling only anger, betrayal, and resignation. She was unaccustomed to being the one asking for support or help in any relationship, and now it was clear why she was so hesitant to do so. The rejection hurt more than she wanted to admit.

The sheet music for Rebecca Clarke's "Passacaglia" was still open on her stand from this morning's practice. It was one of her favorite short pieces, one she usually played as a warm-up in her practice sessions and one she had performed when she auditioned for the Seattle Symphony. The conductor and executive director had remembered, and today, when they learned that the symphony's first-chair violist had injured her wrist, they had called her to the office and offered her the chance to sub for the position for the rest of the year, until a formal audition could be scheduled. The promotion included a rare chance at a viola solo. The symphony was scheduled to give a performance devoted to women composers, and Clarke's sonata for viola and piano had been chosen to open the concert. Since they were bringing in a guest conductor for the evening, the management wanted to showcase local female talent for the solo parts.

Andy knew this was the opportunity of her career, but she had doubts about her ability not only to lead the section as principal viola but to play a solo part in front of a huge audience. Much of the reason she had chosen to play this particular instrument was because she mainly played harmony, background to other instruments, filling out and adding depth to the sound of the orchestra. She had been content in that role for so many years, but the thought of taking on a new challenge appealed to her. Her quartet had been excited when she told them the news at tonight's rehearsal, so she had called Lyssa, hoping that after all of her time spent encouraging the violinist she might be prepared to offer something to Andy in return. What had she been expecting? Support, congratulations, words of advice? Certainly not what she had been given. She wasn't surprised by Lyssa's claim that she was too busy to meet for drinks, but her response to Andy's news about the sonata had caught her off guard.

"They asked *you* to play the solo? I'm surprised you want to step out of the background and risk making a fool of yourself with that piece," Lyssa had said. "There's an alternative cello part for that sonata, so Diane could play it instead. Or maybe they could change the program and let you do one or two of Clarke's shorter songs."

Maybe she was right. Andy had spent most of her career playing beyond the limelight, so was she really ready to make her solo debut on this scale? She considered calling Tina for some moral support, but she knew she would end up confessing how Lyssa's words had hurt. She wasn't prepared to deal with an "I told you so" followed by the inevitable reference to the loyal dog who's been kicked by its uncaring master.

The phone rang and Andy jumped for it, hating the tiny thrill of hope that Lyssa was calling back to apologize.

"Hello?" she repeated when the line remained quiet.

"Is this Andy? It's Brooke Stanton."

"Brooke?" Andy's mind raced, and then the name clicked. October Fifth. Beautiful blonde. Long legs. "Is there a problem about tomorrow?"

"Yes. No, not really. I just wanted to talk about the music we picked."

Christ, thought Andy, running her hand through her hair in exasperation. She knew she had told Brooke that the quartet practiced on Thursdays. There was no way they'd have time to learn something new before tomorrow's rehearsal

"Would it be possible to get together tonight?" Brooke continued.

"Of course," Andy said. *The perfect way to end this day,* she thought with a frown. Why couldn't Brooke have played the Bridezilla card just two days earlier? "Where should we meet?"

"Oh, I'm not sure," Brooke hesitated. "Do you have a bar you like to go to?"

"I sometimes hang out at Mickey's in Pioneer Square, but it's a—"

"That's fine," Brooke cut in quickly. "Say in an hour?"

"Sounds good," Andy answered, but Brooke had already hung up. She stared at the receiver for a moment before replacing it. Andy had been about to tell her Mickey's was big on the local gay scene, but if Brooke wanted to be rude then she could just deal with it. Maybe she'd panic when she found out and cut their meeting short. The thought of a few drinks and the possibility of finding some female company was suddenly very appealing to Andy. Just get through those few uncomfortable minutes with October Fifth, and the night might hold some promise.

"Problems with the wedding plans?" Jake asked as he bent to kiss the top of Brooke's head.

"Not really. I just need to meet with someone from the quartet to finalize the program of music at the church." Brooke hastily closed her binder but not before Jake caught a glimpse of the paper inside.

"Andy? Should I be jealous of him?" Jake teased as he loosened his tie and started unbuttoning his dress shirt.

"He's a she," Brooke said, not really answering his question and turning away so he couldn't read her expression.

"I was hoping you might go out with friends tonight. I hate to be having all the fun while you do more work for the wedding." He replaced his work clothes with a more casual shirt and slacks. "You're sure you don't mind this bachelor party?"

"Not at all," Brooke assured him honestly. "And don't worry about me. I'll be fine."

Jake kissed her again and then disappeared into their bathroom. Brooke slumped onto the bed, still not convinced she could go through with this. She had been determined to forget about women, especially the dark-haired musician who had been haunting her fantasies for the past week, but this afternoon had broken her resolve. It was such a simple thing, really, but it had shaken her to the core.

She ran through the afternoon's conversation again, hoping it wouldn't affect her the same way upon reflection so she could just call Andy and cancel their meeting. She and Jake had gone to lunch with her father, stealing away from his law firm for a leisurely two-hour break. She had picked at her food, barely listening to most of the talk as her dad discussed her parents' plans to retire to the Olympic Peninsula in the next few years. Jake had innocently turned to her and said they should start looking for a retirement condo to buy while the real estate market was in a slump. Her dad agreed that it was never too soon to make plans, and they had spent the rest of lunch discussing the pros and cons of the various small towns along Highway 101. Brooke had sat, quiet and stunned, with the phrase "What the fuck?" running through her head like an unsuccessful mantra. She could barely wrap her mind around the fact that she was getting married, and they already had her retiring with this man? She had been so focused on the wedding itself, she had been able to ignore the years of marriage to follow. It had seemed easiest to go along with her parents' wishes and marry Jake, just like she had accepted him as their choice in prom dates. But instead of being left with a photo and a dried-up corsage, she'd be stuck with the man himself for the rest of her life.

Yes, the memory of the conversation still could trigger hyperventilation. Brooke didn't call Andy back and cancel their appointment. She numbly kissed Jake good-bye, half hoping he might fall in love with a stripper and call off the wedding. Then she carefully got ready to meet Andy, determined to have at least one good night before she settled into the life that Jake and her parents had planned for her. She only had one night, she had to make it count.

CHAPTER FOUR

Mickey's was packed with the usual after-work crowd, but the moment Andy walked through the door she spotted Brooke sitting at the bar. Her blond hair was out of its ponytail, just brushing her shoulders, and she had on jeans and a black tank top in place of business clothes. *Much better,* Andy thought with appreciation as she pushed through the crowd. Andy kept an emotional distance from the brides she met, even the sexier ones, but October Fifth had forced her way into Andy's dreams a time or two this week. She wasn't supposed to feel glad to see this woman who had dragged her out of the house on a bad night. Brooke's attention seemed focused on a lesbian couple across the bar from her, and she jumped when Andy tapped her on the shoulder.

"Hey," Andy said, smiling in spite of her irritation as Brooke's face lit up when she turned around.

"You recognized me without the bridal notebook," Brooke said with a grin.

"You're not easy to forget," Andy admitted. She gestured at the large diamond solitaire on Brooke's left hand. "And that kind of gave you away in this place."

Brooke twisted the ring as if she wanted to pull it off her finger, but she dropped her hands back to cup her drink. "You look nice," she said to Andy, letting her gaze move down the entire length of her. Khaki cargo pants and a clean white T-shirt were as formal as Andy had been willing to go tonight, business meeting or not.

"You, too," Andy said. "This suits you much better than that business outfit did." She reached out without thinking and ran a finger over the strap of Brooke's tank top. *Jesus,* she berated herself when she realized what she was doing. *Stop flirting with the client!* She casually moved her hand away and leaned across Brooke to order a drink when the bartender stopped by.

"Mac and Jack's," she said, ordering her favorite local microbrew. "And another"—she pointed at Brooke's drink—"gin and tonic?"

Brooke nodded, her eyes darkening to the color of faded denim as she watched Andy.

Both seats next to her were taken, so Andy scanned the room looking for a table while they waited for their drinks. She felt Brooke's gaze, but she tried to ignore it and compose herself. She just had to get rid of the bride, and then she would be free to flirt with someone else. Someone who was unattached.

"Careful," Brooke warned as she hooked a finger in the waistband of Andy's pants and pulled her closer. Andy narrowly missed being struck by the man on the stool next to them as he swung his arm around while he was talking.

"Oops, sorry babe," he said over his shoulder.

"No problem," Andy answered without looking at him. Her eyes were locked with Brooke's as she found herself standing inches away from her, nestled between her parted legs. "Thanks," she mumbled, trying to figure out what was going on here. Brooke just watched her, her fingers still tucked in the top of Andy's pants. *Move away,* Andy told herself sternly, *for God's sake move away from her!*

The bartender returned with their drinks, and Andy took that opportunity to extricate herself. She tossed some bills on the counter and picked up her beer and Brooke's cocktail.

"There's a table over there," she nodded toward the wall farthest from the dance floor. She walked off without a backward glance. She sat in a chair with her back against the wall, and Brooke took the seat across from her. *Back to business,* Andy told herself firmly, trying to ignore the sad expression that had come over Brooke's face. "You wanted to talk about the music for your wedding?" she asked, taking a sip of her cold beer.

"I'm doing this all wrong, aren't I?" Brooke asked, ignoring Andy's question.

"Honey, I don't know what the hell you're doing," Andy admitted in exasperation, wincing as she heard herself use that endearment. She had come here tonight expecting to deal with a bitch of a client, and instead she had been nearly pulled into said client's lap. And now Brooke looked ready to cry. She had had enough crap to deal with herself today, she didn't need a ride on some overwrought woman's emotional rollercoaster.

"Look, I know the days before the wedding can be an overwhelming time for a bride," she continued, in what she hoped was a more soothing tone of voice. "Is there someone I can call for you? Your mom, or a bridesmaid?"

"God no," Brooke said with a burst of laughter. "I'm not having a breakdown, you idiot. I'm trying to seduce you."

"Really?" Andy asked in disbelief.

Brooke rolled her eyes. "Thank you. I didn't realize I would be so bad at this." She squeezed lime into her drink with a vengeance, flinging a piece of pulp across the table into Andy's eye.

"Ouch!" she said. Brooke glared at her and Andy scowled back. "You were aiming at me."

Brooke didn't deny it, and Andy had a feeling the rest of the drink might be coming at her if she wasn't careful. She raised her hands in surrender. "No big deal. I'm fine."

Brooke tossed her the condensation-soaked napkin that had been serving as her coaster and stared at the wall behind Andy as she dabbed at her eye.

They sat in silence for several minutes as Andy concentrated on smoothing out the damp napkin, searching for a way to let this apparently distraught woman down gently.

"Look at me?" she finally said, waiting until Brooke dragged her gaze back to meet Andy's. "I don't know what's going on with you tonight. Maybe you have cold feet, or you got in a fight with your fiancé, or he's getting a hooker for his bachelor party and you want revenge. If you need to talk about it, I'll listen. If you want to get drunk, I'll buy. But having sex with a random stranger just because I mentioned I'm a lesbian will not solve your problems."

"Just because…" Brooke started, then stopped. She moved into the chair next to Andy with a bang. "I did *not* call you tonight *just because* you said you were gay. I called because I couldn't get you out of my mind. Because you're so damned gorgeous I haven't stopped thinking about you all week. Because I've been fantasizing about those hands of yours touching me…"

Her voice broke with a vulnerability that tore at Andy's heart, so when Brooke leaned in and kissed her tentatively on the mouth, she only hesitated a heartbeat before she wrapped her fingers in Brooke's hair and pulled her closer. *This is definitely not professional conduct,* Andy thought as she finally moved her mouth away from Brooke's. The best thing to do would be to apologize and get out of there. Instead, Andy found herself trailing kisses along Brooke's cheek toward her ear. "I've had some fantasies myself," she murmured, her breath whispering against Brooke's skin, pulling a quiet moan from her throat.

"Your place?" Brooke asked, raising a hand to lightly touch Andy's lips. Andy simply nodded, then grasped Brooke's hand and pulled her to her feet.

❖

Andy kept her eyes on the BMW in her rearview mirror, thinking that the odds of Brooke coming to her senses and peeling off to head for the safety of home were about fifty-fifty. But when she slipped into a parking place near her Capitol Hill apartment building, the sporty car pulled up beside her.

"Take my spot," she told Brooke through the car's open window. She pointed at the tiny lot of reserved parking stalls. "Number three."

They didn't touch or talk as Andy let them into the building and led the way to her apartment. Once inside she turned to face Brooke, ready to offer a drink or small talk to make her more comfortable.

But before she could speak, Brooke stepped closer and ran her hands through Andy's hair, pulling her head down for a searing kiss.

Andy backed her up against the door, reaching behind them to lock the dead bolt as she ran her tongue across Brooke's lower lip, seeking an opening. Brooke obliged, parting her lips and deepening the kiss without loosening her hold on Andy's head. She broke the contact suddenly, slipping out from under Andy's arms and backing down the narrow hallway.

"Bedroom?" she asked, pulling her tank top over her head and letting it fall to the floor. Andy followed slowly, mimicking Brooke's actions and tugging off her T-shirt.

"End of the hall," she said, not sure if she could catch her breath enough for a complete sentence as she watched Brooke slip out of her bra. She followed suit and unhooked hers as they entered the small room. Brooke kept backing up, her eyes never leaving Andy's, until her legs bumped against the bed. Andy stopped when she did, still several feet away, and watched with anticipation as Brooke moved her hands down to the button of her jeans, slowly sliding them down her legs. Pink underwear followed. Only then did Andy remove her own pants, wanting to let Brooke take the lead. Even if it killed her, she wanted to be ready to stop if Brooke came to her senses and changed her mind.

Luckily she didn't, and Andy breathed a sigh of relief as Brooke came into her arms and pressed the full length of her soft body against Andy's more muscular one. She cried out against Andy's lips as she moved against her, rubbing breasts against breasts, her curly triangle against Andy's pubic mound. Andy moved her lips down Brooke's throat to her breasts, stopping only to impatiently toss the covers aside before lowering her to the bed.

Brooke captured Andy's mouth again and flipped them over until she was straddling her. She rained kisses on Andy's neck and mouth as she slid against her. "God, the feel of you…" she groaned as she settled onto her side next to Andy.

Andy lay as still as she could while Brooke watched her own hands roam across Andy's breasts and stomach. Brooke had a slightly dazed and surprised look on her face, and Andy wondered how much of that was due to being in bed with another woman or simply with someone other than her fiancé. Either way, she ran her hands gently along Brooke's spine, not wanting to frighten her away with any aggressive movements until she was certain Brooke was comfortable. But even her tentative touches and feather-light kisses were enough to make Andy tremble with desire. She had to fight harder to keep control than she ever had with more experienced lovers. Finally Brooke's hand reached down to trail lightly through Andy's slick curls, making her moan and arch toward the brief contact.

"You're so wet," Brooke's breath was ragged and her tone amazed as their eyes met. Andy almost drowned in those eyes, glistening like crystals with the intensity of Brooke's desire. "I...I want to taste you. Is that all right?"

"Is it all right? Are you fucking kidding me?" Andy rasped out.

Brooke laughed, her nervousness dissolving as she saw Andy's obvious hunger for her. She watched Andy's face as she slipped fingers between her legs with more confidence. She dragged her wet fingers up Andy's torso and swirled them around Andy's taut nipple before lowering her head to suck and taste her. Andy cried out and arched her back, pushing her breast deeper into Brooke's mouth. Brooke obliged, sucking harder before she raised her head again.

"Mmm," she purred. "So sweet."

Brooke slowly kissed her way down the wet trail on Andy's stomach, surprised she felt so comfortable taking control. From her first shy kiss in the bar to the short drive as she followed Andy home, Brooke's uncertainty had gradually vanished and had been replaced with a sense that she had made the right decision and this was the right place for her to be. She paused at Andy's lower abdomen, drawing her tongue across the strong muscles and making Andy groan and open her legs in invitation. Brooke felt trembling fingers gently rake through her hair, encouraging her to move lower.

"Please, Brooke, please," Andy begged, gasping as Brooke's mouth finally found her inner folds. Brooke had expected to feel unsure, to need Andy to explain what to do, but the way Andy's body responded to her tongue's gentle exploration gave her an unanticipated sense of connection. She had never realized that a lover's arousal could so directly lead to her own. Her self-consciousness slowly changed to curiosity, then confidence, then hunger. Her tongue grew more determined, and it only took one firm brush across Andy's swollen clit to make her come with a sharp cry that gave Brooke all the reassurance she needed.

Brooke laughed with delight and scooted up the bed to rain kisses along Andy's neck and pull her into her arms.

"You liked that, I take it?" Andy asked, pulling Brooke's mouth to hers.

"That was amazing. I could feel so much energy building up in you, and I had the key to release it." She flicked her tongue across Andy's lower lip.

She gasped then as Andy quickly nipped at that tongue and sucked it into her own mouth. "You think that was amazing?" she asked as she flipped Brooke onto her back. "It gets even better," she growled, pinning Brooke's wrists above her head as she kissed her way down Brooke's throat. Brooke kept her hands raised, her fists clenched, even as Andy let go of them in order to use both mouth and fingers to tease her full breasts. Using all of her skill, she sucked and rubbed until Brooke was moaning and writhing with passion underneath her. Andy dropped a hand to Brooke's thigh and sucked a nipple into her mouth, grazing it with her teeth as she entered Brooke hard with two fingers.

"Oh God!" Brooke yelled in surprise, pushing with her hips onto Andy's hand and tangling her fingers in Andy's hair.

That was all the invitation Andy needed. She quickly moved between Brooke's legs, pumping with her fingers in time to the rhythm of thrusting hips and letting her lips and tongue feast on her sweet wetness.

Brooke seemed ready to climax, but Andy forced herself to slow down, easing the pressure of her fingers so she could enjoy her exploration of Brooke's slick folds. She held out as long as she could, loving the taste of her and the rapid rise and fall of Brooke's breathing. Finally a whimpered "Andy, please!" urged her to move to Brooke's swollen clit, sucking it into her mouth and gently grazing against it with her teeth. Her fingers resumed their determined rhythm and her tongue matched it, flicking rapidly over Brooke's clit.

Brooke came, quietly gasping, and then sagged back against the bed. *Oh no you don't,* Andy thought, sensing that Brooke was holding back, trying to control her body's responses. She sucked more firmly, shifting the position of her fingers as she continued to fuck Brooke until she came again, crying out with abandon this time, her defenses too weak to deny herself a full release.

Andy quickly moved to her side, pulling the covers with her and drawing them around Brooke's trembling shoulders. She gently kissed her salty tears.

"I know," she murmured, holding her close. "It's not easy to let go like that the first time."

Brooke sniffed and snuggled deeper into Andy's arms. Andy stroked her back, loving the feeling of their bodies as they molded together, trying to ignore the diamond that still glinted on Brooke's finger.

CHAPTER FIVE

Andy slid her hand across the cool sheets, sensing even in her half-awake state that Brooke had left her bed. She rolled onto her back and stared at the ceiling, afraid to get up and look for a note. Last night had been incredible, and Andy couldn't remember the last time she had shared such a physical connection with another woman. The give and take, the ability to sense what the other wanted and to adapt to meet her demands, the conflict between her body's responses to Brooke's explorations and her desire to turn the tables and get her hands and mouth on Brooke again.

She finally got out of bed and pulled on a pair of sweatpants and a tank top. Brooke had gathered Andy's clothes off the floor and had stacked them haphazardly on a bedroom chair, but other than that small attempt at housekeeping there were no signs that she had been in the apartment at all last night. Andy walked through her small space twice, searching in vain for some acknowledgment from Brooke. She glanced at the clock and then went to find Brooke's paperwork to get her phone number. It wasn't quite eight, but Andy needed to talk to her and find out what was going on. There was no way Brooke could have shared herself with Andy like that and still be planning on marrying someone else. She must be dealing with her family and her fiancé, and although Andy hated to interrupt, she knew Brooke would need her support today.

A cheerful male voice answered the phone on the second ring. He didn't sound like the distraught fiancé, and Andy held the phone in silence for a moment.

"Hello?" he asked again.

"Is Brooke there?" Andy managed.

"No, she went to brunch with her bridesmaids. Can I help you with something?"

Andy didn't know how to respond to that. *No, I just fucked your fiancée last night and I wanted to call and see how she's doing.* "That's okay, thanks. I had a question about the music for the service, but I guess it's no big deal."

"Is this Andy?" Jake asked. Andy managed a surprised affirmation. "Brooke told me she was meeting with you last night. Did everything go all right?"

"Everything went fine." *All right? Fine? How about, there were fireworks. The earth moved.* "I'll see both of you at the church then."

"Sounds great. I'm looking forward to meeting you." Jake hung up, sparing Andy the necessity of lying and saying she was looking forward to any part of the day, especially meeting the man who was marrying Brooke. She spent the next half hour in a scalding hot shower, trying to force some feeling back into her suddenly numbed body.

❖

Brooke sat passively in the midst of a bustle of activity as the hairstylist fussed with her blond curls. Jake's sister Emily twirled around her, making the skirt of her flower girl dress stand straight out. Bridesmaids laughed and talked as they waited their turn for the seamstress to do a last-minute fitting, and Brooke's mom and the florist debated whether to add an extra flower arrangement at the altar. Brooke glanced at the mass of white satin hanging on the back of the door. Soon she would need to put it on and stand still while the seamstress measured and pinned. One step closer to getting married.

From the outside, Brooke knew she looked like the calmest person in the room, but inside her thoughts were in turmoil. Being with Andy had raised so many questions, instead of simply satisfying a curiosity as she had expected it to. She felt powerless to stop the preparations going on around her, but she had to admit she was the one who had put these events in motion. She had accepted Jake's proposal, she had planned the details of the wedding. Now it had a momentum of its own, and Brooke couldn't find a way to stop the wave of activity as it pulled her toward the altar. She wasn't even sure she wanted to.

Her face hurt from smiling at all the people who congratulated her and said how happy they were to share this most important event of her life. They had no idea how insignificant the wedding seemed compared to the life-changing night she had shared with Andy. She was left alone to dwell on the implications of her body's responses to another woman's touch, but the constant barrage of wedding details made it difficult to process her feelings about Andy, about their lovemaking. She had wanted to talk to Andy early in the morning, to wake her up and admit to a rising panic as she contemplated getting married, but she had been too scared. Scared to acknowledge those feelings, scared to discover that maybe their night together hadn't meant as much to Andy as it had to her.

Brooke checked her watch. Her friend Jan should be arriving soon from Spokane. She was the only person Brooke could confide in right now. Even though her mom didn't approve of their friendship, Brooke had insisted on inviting Jan to the rehearsal and the dinner following it. It was the only battle Brooke had fought in all of her wedding preparations, acquiescing to her mother in every other instance.

Finally the last flower was pinned into her elaborate hairstyle, and Brooke allowed herself to be cinched into the white gown. She stared blankly at her reflection as the seamstress checked the fit and everyone else made the appropriate compliments due to a bride. All Brooke could see when she looked in the mirror was the cost of the dress. Thousands of dollars for this custom gown, and numerous nonrefundable payments to other vendors would be lost if she called off the wedding now. Plus the embarrassment her family would experience as they tried to explain her change of heart, the wasted time for everyone who had helped her with plans, and—most of all—the pain she would cause Jake if she walked away from him.

Brooke felt some relief when she turned around so the seamstress could check her train. She knew the real reason she was afraid to cancel the wedding, and she hated facing herself in the mirror because of it. Everyone she loved seemed convinced that marrying Jake was the right choice for her. She had defied her family's wishes once before, and the results had been disastrous. How could she claim to know the right choice now? How could she put everything that mattered to her at risk because of one fantastic night with Andy? Her parents would recover from the lost expenses and the humiliation, her friends and family would go on with their lives, and Jake would survive without her. The real cost of cancelling the wedding would be faced by Brooke herself. Her way of life, her family, her friends. They all could be lost if Brooke left Jake and came out as a lesbian. She didn't know Andy, didn't know how she felt about their night together. She couldn't expect her to step in as family, to single-handedly replace everyone Brooke loved. If she walked away from the wedding, she might be walking all alone. That was a price she wasn't willing to pay.

Andy walked into the church well before the rehearsal was scheduled to start. She looked for Brooke but the florist told her the bridal party hadn't arrived yet. Andy kept herself busy arranging the chairs for the quartet and playing some quiet scales on her viola. She hadn't been able to concentrate during her regular morning practice, and her hands were shaking so badly that even her simple scales were played with vibrato. She alternated between anger at letting herself be used for a fling and frustration because she had glimpsed the possibility of something beautiful and had it snatched away.

The other three members of her quartet came up the aisle together and settled in their usual seats. David turned to Andy and launched into one of his routine pre-wedding jokes, but his voice faded to a stop when he met her eyes.

"Shit, darling, who died?" he asked.

Richard shook his head in disapproval. "Her self-respect did."

"Not Lyssa again?" Tina asked. "She give you a rough night?"

"I haven't seen Lyssa in a week," Andy said, rosining her bow for the fourth time since she had arrived at the church. She took a soft cloth out of her case and gently wiped off the excess. "Did you notice if the bride is here yet?" she asked nonchalantly.

No one answered immediately, and Andy looked up from her bow to find the three of them staring at her.

"'The bride?' Oh my God," Tina gasped. "You slept with October Fifth!"

Andy stared at her, too shocked that anyone could have guessed her secret to formulate a denial. "Shut up," she said, glancing at the sanctuary doors to make sure no one could have overheard Tina's loud statement.

"You really will do anything to keep the brides happy, won't you, Andy dear?" David laughed with delight. Richard seemed too stunned to speak.

"All of you, shut up!" Andy repeated. "I'll be right back."

She started up the aisle, but Tina followed and grabbed her arm. She spoke in a low voice. "Seriously, Andy, tell me you didn't."

Andy just shook her head and stared up at a stained-glass window. She wasn't a regular at church, but she had a pretty good idea that her conduct didn't fall in the acceptable category. "It just happened," she finally admitted. "I met Brooke last night at Mickey's, and we sort of ended up going back to my place."

"She was at Mickey's? She's a lesbian?"

"No. I don't know," Andy said. "She called and said she wanted to talk, and that's where I was going."

"Oh," Tina said with an understanding nod. "She was looking for one last great orgasm before settling down for fifty years of marriage. Typical curious straight girl, I suppose, looking for her fun and then it's over. Been there. Would she even touch you?" she asked with curiosity.

"God, Tina, it wasn't like that at all." Brooke may have been inexperienced, but she was certainly not selfish. And after a little practice she had handled Andy's body like a pro. Andy felt her cheeks redden slightly under Tina's scrutiny.

Tina's voice changed with sympathy. "You've got it bad, don't you. How is she feeling about all of this?"

"She left early this morning," Andy said, running a hand through her hair in frustration. "I need to talk to her before the rehearsal."

"Go," Tina said, giving her a little push toward the doors. "I'll stay here and administer CPR to Richard. He expects this kind of behavior from me, not you, Ms. Propriety."

Andy pushed through the growing crowd of guests and, after questioning a woman in a lilac silk dress who appeared to be a bridesmaid, found herself at the door of the Sunday school room that was being used for the bridal party. She hesitated before knocking, unsure about the reaction she would get from Brooke. Indifference? Tears? Regret? She didn't know this woman, not really, but she knew from experience that a connection like this didn't come along every day, or every lifetime. They couldn't just walk away from it without at least discussing what had happened between the two of them. Feeling more sure of herself, Andy finally knocked on the door.

An older woman answered her knock, clearly disapproving of the interruption. "Yes, can I help you?"

Brooke's mother, Andy figured. She was about to ask for Brooke when she looked past the woman and saw her standing by the window with another couple of bridesmaids. Andy had seen her share of brides in wedding gowns, many of them admittedly sexy, but she had never had one take her breath away. Even in the incongruous setting with its tiny chairs and posters of cartoon Bible scenes and scriptures on the walls, Brooke was gorgeous. The strapless dress was heavy with beadwork and flared out slightly at her hips, accentuating the curves and softness that Andy remembered so well. Her mouth suddenly felt dry, and she stood staring at the bride while her traitorous mind wondered how she could get Brooke out of that dress without resorting to scissors.

"It's all right, Mom," Brooke said smoothly. "Andy is a friend of mine. Her quartet is playing today. Can you give us a few minutes to talk?"

Brooke's mother's gaze swept over Andy, taking in her short hair and the black satin pantsuit with the open-collared tuxedo shirt underneath that was her standard wedding attire. Fitted enough to look slightly feminine, it made no pretense of being girly. Andy could almost hear the judgments being formed in the woman's mind as she reluctantly stepped aside to let Andy enter the room.

"I'll be right outside if you need me, darling," she said to Brooke as she and the other women left.

Andy and Brooke stared at each other for a long moment. Brooke's eyes were icy blue again in the autumn sunlight that streamed through the window, and Andy couldn't read any expression in them.

Finally she cleared her throat self-consciously. "What does she think I'm going to do to you?" she asked, gesturing with her head toward the door.

"Don't be silly," Brooke said, maintaining that maddeningly aloof air. "She just wants to be sure nothing spoils the day."

"And I might spoil it?" Andy asked with sadness.

Brooke shook her head, whether in denial or irritation Andy couldn't tell. "Why are you here?"

"To play my viola at your wedding rehearsal."

"Don't," Brooke said sharply. "Why are you here?" she repeated, gesturing around the room.

Andy sighed in frustration. This day, and this conversation, weren't going at all as she had expected. She took a step toward Brooke, needing to know that this ice princess was the same warm woman who had shared her bed last night. Brooke had half a step to back up before she bumped into the wall, and Andy saw a flicker of worry in her eyes. At least that was something. She finished crossing the empty space between them and raised a finger to trace along the neckline of Brooke's dress.

"Jesus," she breathed. "You are so beautiful."

Brooke inhaled sharply at her touch and raised her hand to Andy's. She meant to push her away, but instead their fingers entwined, and she pressed their joined hands to her breast.

She didn't resist when Andy leaned forward and their lips met. The kiss seared her soul, bringing back all of the passion from the night before in a rush. When Andy moved her mouth away, Brooke gave a ragged cry of protest that turned to a sigh as Andy rained kisses along her collarbone and over the slight swell of her breasts.

Brooke laced her fingers in Andy's soft hair, tugging to bring her mouth back to her own. She parted her lips, and when Andy's tongue slid into her mouth she sagged against the wall feeling a rush of wanting, of wetness.

"No. No!" she gasped. She had struggled all day to strengthen her resolve to marry Jake, but having Andy so close, touching her, threatened all of Brooke's carefully reasoned arguments for going through with the wedding. She needed space if she was going to stay strong, and she pushed Andy's shoulders away. Her hands felt too weak to be effective, but Andy stepped back at the light touch. They both raised fingers to their lips as if in disbelief at their own responses.

"Tell me that means nothing to you, that you don't feel anything when I touch you," Andy said. Brooke glanced at the door, worried her mother would hear even though Andy kept her voice low. Her breathing was fast, her throat warm from Andy's kisses and her own arousal. She remained silent, though, and Andy pushed on.

"I know last night was your first time with a woman, but you have to realize that what we shared was special. How can you just turn your back on it like it didn't happen?"

Brooke's eyes flashed with anger. "But one night of sex and you expect me to turn my back on Jake, on my family? A couple of orgasms and you want me to walk away from a fiancé who loves me, a church full of my friends and family, a wedding that cost thousands of dollars?"

"It was more than that and you know it," Andy said, her hands gentle as she slid them along Brooke's waist even though her voice was rough with emotion. "There's something between us, and I think we should explore it. All I'm asking is some time for us to—"

"To what?" Brooke spit out angrily. "To date? Sorry, Jake, but we need to postpone the wedding so I can go for dinner and a movie with one of the musicians. Would your quartet give us a discount if we reschedule?"

Andy dropped her hands and stepped away from Brooke again. "Uncalled for," she said, her eyes full of sorrow.

Brooke wouldn't let herself be swayed. She hated to watch herself hurt Andy, but there was no other way to make her leave. Brooke had gotten an answer to a question she had wondered about repeatedly today, she thought to herself bitterly. She now knew Andy was as moved by last night as she had been. But she couldn't risk trusting her own judgment again, no matter how much her body protested. "I am not a lesbian. Nothing will change that fact, even if I wasn't getting married tomorrow."

Andy snorted. "I guess the big white dress and the male groom should have tipped me off," she said, crossing her arms over her chest. "I must have been confused by the way you were screaming my name last night."

"I would deny that, but I'm sure your neighbors can corroborate your story," Brooke said with as much dignity as she could muster.

Andy looked at the bride in amazement. "That was a joke?" she asked in disbelief, a small smile playing over her lips. Brooke shrugged, carefully schooling her features to keep her answering smile hidden.

"So what was it?" Andy asked, more softly this time. "A fling? Curiosity? A sexy story to tell Jake some day?"

"All of those, I guess," Brooke admitted, looking out the window. She turned her head and gazed directly into Andy's eyes. "But you shattered me," she said, so quietly that Andy barely could hear. "I knew it would feel good to be with you, but you shattered me."

Andy reached out, but Brooke shook her head and sidestepped her touch. There was a quick tap on the door before it opened, and Brooke's mother stuck her head inside.

"Darling, we really need to start the rehearsal," she said, glancing from Brooke to Andy. "Is everything all right?"

Brooke didn't seem able to speak, so for the second time that day Andy answered that question with a lie.

"Everything is fine."

❖

Andy somehow made it through the rehearsal, relying on muscle memory and habit to get her through the luckily familiar music. She faltered only once, when Brooke appeared at the head of the aisle with her father. She had changed from her wedding gown to a rose-colored dress that matched the flush Andy had brought to her skin when, only minutes before, she had scattered kisses across a soft, bare throat. Tina kicked her in the shin, and she jolted back to awareness in time to join the quartet for the wedding march. She kept her face composed while Brooke quietly but steadily recited her vows and pretended to slip a ring on Jake's finger. She imagined Tina watching her with sympathy, Richard with anxiousness, and David with hopeful anticipation, but she managed to remain silent when the minister asked if there were any objections, keeping her eyes focused on Brooke's back. She raised her viola and joined the others as they played the measured beats of Beethoven for the recessional, unable to watch Brooke walk away from the altar on Jake's arm.

CHAPTER SIX

B rooke wasn't sure how she made it through the rehearsal without fainting. She could feel Andy's eyes on her the entire time, and she couldn't make herself look at the quartet when they played. If their gazes met, she knew she would no longer be able to control her expression. Jake, her family, everyone would see what she felt for this woman who was virtually a stranger to her. So she did what she did best and let her mind disconnect from her surroundings and let her body endure the mock ceremony, as if on autopilot. It was easier than usual since no part of her felt familiar, from her professionally done hair and makeup to the stiffly formal dress she wore.

Last night hadn't felt familiar either, yet it had seemed so natural to be with Andy, to touch her and taste her, to open herself up to this unknown woman. If they had met under different circumstances, maybe they could have tried to form a relationship out of their mutual attraction. But Brooke stood in the church surrounded by the people closest to her. If she chose to leave Jake, she could lose them all. Her conservative parents and relatives and even the bridal party, most of whom had been friends with Jake before they welcomed her into their circle. Everyone except Jan, who sat alone in the back row. Was it worth it just to embrace an unconventional lifestyle, an unknown future, a sexy violist with gold-flecked hazel eyes that blazed when they looked at her naked body?

Okay, maybe she shouldn't be thinking of words like *naked*, Brooke decided. But while the quartet played "Ave Maria" during a pause in the ceremony, Brooke focused on the viola's deep harmony and allowed her mind to touch gently on the previous night. Cautiously, guarding against a rush of emotion, she let herself remember the less passionate, but oh-so-tender moments. The whisper of Andy's breath as she nuzzled Brooke's ear, the gentle twining of hands as they rested close to each other, the few beautiful minutes of waking up in Andy's arms before she had to slip out of bed and back into her world. She smiled, and Jake grinned back at her, his face full of love and possessiveness.

Brooke passively recited her vows, and she could have been repeating words in Swahili for all she knew. She had a moment of frantic hope that Andy would speak up when the minister asked for objections, but the run-through of the ceremony was concluded without a single discordant note. Before she realized it was over, Jake was kissing her while she fought not to turn her head away. Then a blur of faces as they walked up the aisle, a hug from her tearful mother, a crowd of people with questions about the next day. Brooke suffered through it all with the appropriate smile on her face, but her eyes scanned the room anxiously as she hoped for one final glimpse of Andy.

❖

Brooke picked listlessly at her lasagna, weary from hours of pushing away thoughts of Andy and pretending to be the happy bride. The effort of it all was starting to wear on her, and all she wanted to do was find someplace to sleep.

"What are you doing here?" Evelyn asked sharply, taking the empty chair next to her daughter.

"It's the wedding party's table. I'm eating my dinner," Brooke answered grimly. Apparently her mother's tears and smiles were spent for the night.

"Why are you doing this to me? Can't you look happy for just one day?"

Evelyn tended to turn any sign of her daughter's moodiness into a personal insult. Although Brooke was accustomed to these criticisms, they still managed to make her feel more exhausted than before. It felt like the blood in her veins was turning to lead, and she fought the urge to lay her head on the table and close her eyes. That'd give her mother a stroke.

"I'm just tired," Brooke said, her usual response to her mom's accusations.

"Well, your father spent a lot of money on this rehearsal dinner, and all of these people took the time to come see you. The least you can do is visit with them. Now get up and talk to your Uncle Lewis. Oh, wait, here comes Jake. Do try to act happy for once."

Brooke was relieved to see Jake coming to rescue her from sweaty Uncle Lewis, but that relief was short-lived.

"Brooke, baby, the photographer is waiting for us. I want some pictures of us with my family."

He gestured toward a table where his parents and grandparents were clustered. In a feeling that was all too familiar, her exhaustion lifted and was immediately replaced by anxiety. She wiped suddenly sweaty palms on her dress as she looked around desperately for a way to escape.

"Bathroom," she said, and then repeated in a calmer voice. "I need to go to the bathroom first. I'll hurry," she assured Jake and her mother.

"Is everything all right, dear?" Evelyn asked.

"Of course. Look, there's Jan. She can go with me," Brooke said when she saw her old college roommate heading toward them. Jan had her coat over her arm and was obviously coming to say good-bye, but Brooke grabbed her arm and pulled her toward the front of the restaurant.

"Come with me, please," she whispered, tugging a surprised Jan along with her and ignoring her mother's disapproving stare.

"Where are we going?"

"The bathroom," hissed Brooke.

She led Jan into the handicapped stall and locked the door, sagging against it with a relieved sigh.

Jan looked confused. "So, um, do you need help getting out of that thing?" she asked gamely, plucking at the top layer of Brooke's full skirt. "I've heard those nylons can be tricky."

Brooke lightly swatted her hand away with a short laugh. "I don't need to pee. I just wanted to talk."

"Thank God," Jan said, leaning against the wall facing Brooke. "You look a bit shell-shocked. Do you want me to explain what to expect on your wedding night?" she teased.

Brooke genuinely smiled for the first time that day. "Thanks for coming all this way," she said, ignoring the reference to sex with her husband. She had been surprised that Jan had accepted her invitation, the only one she had sent to anyone from her old college days. "It means a lot to me."

Jan shrugged. "It's only a five-hour drive from Spokane. It was worth it to see you so…happy? Is that the look you're going for?"

Brooke grimaced. "Of course I'm happy. Thrilled, as a matter of fact. The luckiest woman in the world."

Jan laughed and held up her hands in surrender. "Well, you've certainly convinced me." She shook her head sadly and her voice became serious. "All right, spill it."

"I cheated on Jake. Last night."

"Jesus," Jan said. "What's her name?"

"What makes you think it's a woman?"

"Come on, you're talking to me, not your mother or one of your prissy bridesmaids."

"I'm sorry I didn't ask you to…" Brooke wavered. Jan was the closest she had to a friend, but her mother had never approved of her lifestyle and would have been horrified if Brooke had asked her to be in the wedding.

"Don't worry about it," Jan waved her hand in dismissal. "I kind of figured your family would prefer a non-gay wedding party. Now what's her name?"

"Andy," Brooke admitted, feeling a little thrill at saying her name out loud. "The viola player from the quartet."

"The quartet that's playing for your ceremony? You do have a flair for the dramatic." Jan laughed and shook her head. "And I'll admit you have excellent taste. She's beautiful."

Brooke stared at the hands she had clasped in front of her. "I know," she said quietly.

"So," Jan prompted. "How was it?"

Brooke met her eyes and sighed.

"Uh-oh."

"What am I going to do?" Brooke whispered. "It was so... amazing. I've never felt anything like it. But I hardly know her, and I can't just walk away from my life."

"How does Andy feel about this?"

"She came to see me before the rehearsal. I think she wants us to...date. To try."

"I'm sorry it happened like this," Jan said. "Maybe it would have been better if you had never experienced sex with a woman. Then you wouldn't know what you'll be missing."

Brooke's tears finally started to fall. "No. I'd never give up last night. No matter how much it hurts."

Jan ripped off some toilet paper and gently wiped her friend's face. "It's never too late, Brooke. I know a lot of people would be hurt if you cancelled the wedding, but is it better to tell Jake now, or to live a life of regret and lies with him? Do you really think you can be happy with him now that you know?"

"It's too hard to leave, to change."

"It would have been easier if you had just gone out with me when I asked in college instead of trying to deny you were a lesbian." She laughed and pulled Brooke into a tight hug. "Is this a bad time to say 'I told you so'?"

"What should I do?" Brooke whispered.

Jan moved out of the hug but kept her hands on Brooke's shoulders. "Do you want assurances that everything is fine the way it is, or do you want the truth?"

"The truth?" Brooke said, uncertainly.

"All right then. Drop the Maid Marian act. Stop waiting for someone else to make decisions for you. Stop trying to be rescued. Decide what's right for you and how you want to live your life and go for it. You're doing the same thing you did in college. So you had your heart broken, it's happened to all of us. But instead of picking yourself up and going on, you ran away and surrendered your whole life to Mommy and Daddy. Now you're going to marry a man you don't love the right way, and you're pretending to be someone you're not. Either shut up and deal with it, or grow a backbone and rescue yourself for a change."

"Wow," Brooke said quietly when she could speak again. "How long have you been waiting to say that?"

"Since you packed up and left college," Jan replied with a laugh. "And it felt good. Look, it's not always easy to be true to who you are. I certainly know that from my own experience. But even though your family and friends may not approve of your choices, you'll feel a lot more peace inside if you just let yourself be who you are."

"Brooke? Darling?" Evelyn's voice drifted in, her worry undisguised. "Are you all right?"

Brooke closed her eyes. She needed more time to choose, to decide. But she had had time. The years between her disgraced return home from college and tomorrow, her wedding day. Months of half-hearted attempts to delay the inevitable ceremony while she waited for some miraculous intervention to save her. None had come, and now it was up to her. She realized that she had already started to take charge when she went home with Andy last night, attempting to snatch a moment of truth in a life of lies.

Brooke grabbed Jan's hands. "I may need a place to stay tonight," she whispered as her mother knocked gently on the stall door. Jan nodded.

"I'll be right outside," she murmured, giving Brooke a quick kiss on the cheek. "Good luck."

Brooke smiled faintly and unlocked the door.

Chapter Seven

Brooke knocked twice on Andy's apartment door even though she had seen her empty parking space in the lot below. After two days of explanations and arguments, Brooke had an overwhelming need to see Andy again, to get some sort of confirmation that she had done the right thing, no matter how painful it had been for everyone involved. Her night with Andy had felt amazing, but it had gone far beyond sex, beyond the joy of being with someone who knew how to touch her, to make love to her. The feelings had gone deeper than her skin, and for that reason alone Brooke had been able to find the strength to face Jake and her parents and call off the wedding.

Or postpone *the wedding,* she thought with a pang of guilt. She had told Jake she needed time to think, to make sure of what she wanted, but she hadn't been able to tell anyone about Andy or her questions about her own sexuality. She prevaricated partly because it was enough of a nightmare to go through the horrible task of explaining the situation to friends and relatives. But the real reason she couldn't admit she might be a lesbian was that she wasn't completely sure herself. Had her night with Andy really been so earthshaking, or had she been looking frantically for an excuse to escape the upcoming wedding? Brooke had to see Andy again, to spend time close to her and discover if her feelings were genuine or imagined.

Brooke sat on the hall's rough carpet, determined to wait for Andy. She knew so little about this woman she was waiting for.

Where she worked, how she spent her time. For all Brooke knew, Andy was on a date right now and wouldn't even come home tonight. Or, worse yet, she would bring the date here only to find a desperate Brooke loitering on her doorstep. Embarrassing as that would be, Brooke couldn't leave now. Jan had been silently supportive over the past two days, even when Brooke's mom launched into her "What did *you* do to her?" attack, but she had returned to her home and job in Spokane. The thought of a lonely hotel room was too depressing, and most of her friends were Jake's as well, so Brooke would have to answer their endless questions with less than complete honesty. She didn't want sympathy or pity or another night of hiding her true feelings. She wanted Andy. Still, when she heard footsteps approaching, she wished there was someplace to hide in the bare hallway. Or at least that she had called Andy herself yesterday, when she went through the exhausting chore of cancelling vendors, instead of making Jan do it.

❖

Andy wearily climbed the stairs to her apartment, wanting nothing more than a long soak in the tub. She had hardly slept the night before, and it had taken all of her concentration to stay awake during the Sunday matinee performance of Mahler's Fifth Symphony. She had put in a few extra hours of practice last night and this morning, mostly to help push images of Brooke out of her mind, and her shoulders ached from the added work.

The past couple of days had reminded Andy why she tried to keep drama out of her life and relationships. Brooke had managed to shake her carefully maintained sense of equilibrium, throwing her from one emotion to the next without time to process any of them. She had felt a sense of awe Thursday night when she and Brooke seemed to come together so effortlessly, but the following days had tossed her into chaos. She had survived the gut-wrenching realization that Brooke was determined to go through with the wedding, only to have it replaced by confusion when some unidentified woman called and said the quartet wouldn't be needed Saturday night. She had spent the afternoon wondering whether Brooke had called off the wedding or whether she didn't want to see Andy again and possibly have a repeat of their confrontation before the rehearsal. She had tried calling once but hadn't left a message, and finally she drove to the church and sat in the empty parking lot. Relief because the wedding was obviously off warred with hurt and sadness since Brooke clearly didn't want to talk to her. Whatever was going on with Brooke, Andy knew she needed to stay far away from her if she wanted to keep her sanity.

It took her tired mind a few seconds to process the silhouettes clustered in the dim hallway outside of her apartment door. She closed her eyes for a moment, but when she opened them again she still saw Brooke, sitting and leaning wearily against the wall with two large suitcases next to her. Brooke rolled her head to the side as she approached, watching her in silence. Andy didn't know what to say. She was foolishly glad to see Brooke again, but now that she was here, there were so many questions Andy didn't know how to start. So she stepped over Brooke's outstretched legs and unlocked her door, picking up one of the suitcases and taking it into her living room. Brooke got up and followed her, hauling the other case and dropping it just inside the hallway.

They stood and looked at each other. *God, I barely know this woman,* Andy realized. "I didn't expect to see you," she finally spoke.

"I left Jake," Brooke said quietly, her eyes icy blue and unrevealing. "I spent the last two nights with a friend, but she had to leave this morning for Spokane. I have nowhere else to go."

"So you want to stay here?" Andy asked in disbelief. She was torn between a rush of desire to drag Brooke to her bedroom for a repeat of Thursday night, and an instinctive impulse to get away from this situation that seemed destined to be messy and disruptive. In just two days, Brooke had managed to upend her emotions, her sleep, and even her practice schedule. Andy didn't want to imagine what damage a full-time relationship with her could cause. "Wouldn't you be better off with your parents or a friend?"

Brooke laughed derisively. "My parents won't speak to me, and most of my friends are Jake's, too, so I'm not comfortable staying with any of them."

"So you want to stay here?" Andy repeated.

Brooke crossed her arms over her chest. "After Thursday night, I figured you owed me at least that much."

"I have to let you move in because the sex was great?"

"No, because you ruined my wedding," Brooke answered.

"I don't know about that," Andy said with a shrug. "A lot of people complimented us on the music."

"Very funny," Brooke rolled her eyes. "You know what I mean."

"No, I don't. You're the one who seduced *me*, then ran away so you could marry a *man* for God's sake. How exactly is this my fault?"

"You came to me Friday. You said you wanted us to have a chance to get to know each other," Brooke spoke quietly, her voice wavering slightly as if she was close to tears. Andy unsuccessfully fought the urge to comfort her, to touch her.

"I wanted you to stop the wedding," she admitted, moving toward Brooke and gently brushing at a strand of honey-blond hair. "I wanted us to be able to start from scratch and get to know each other, to let you figure things out about yourself. But moving in together while you decide what you want is too big a step. I don't want to spend another night with you only to have you leave again. You should go home."

"No," Brooke whispered, closing her eyes as if to block out those words. "I can't go running back again." She met Andy's gaze again. "I don't expect us to..." she gestured toward the bedroom, ignoring the faint rush of heat that flooded her face at the memory of their night together. "I just need a place to stay until I figure out what to do. I thought we could talk, be friends."

Friends, yeah, that would work, Andy thought sarcastically. Just a simple wave toward her bedroom and both of them were blushing like infatuated schoolgirls. She casually took a couple of steps back. "Do they know you're with me?"

Brooke shrugged. "They don't care," she said. "Well, they don't know. It was hard enough to tell them I changed my mind without bringing you into it."

"But you cancelled a wedding. How did you explain it to everyone without mentioning our night together?"

"I just said I needed to decide what I really want out of life before I settle down. And that's true, Andy. I have to take this one step at a time, and the first was to stop the wedding. Once I have time to figure out how I really feel, I can spring the rest on them."

And where will that leave me? Andy wondered. She kept that question to herself. "And Jake?" she asked instead.

"He gave me an ultimatum," Brooke shrugged again. "I have until Christmas to choose between him and…"

"Me?" asked Andy with a frown.

"No, at least not you in particular. Between him and not him."

Andy didn't respond and Brooke tried once more, desperation growing in her voice. "I don't have any place else to go," she repeated. "My dad and Jake are lawyers at the firm where I work, so I don't want to go back there. I don't have a job, a home…"

She stopped and raised shaking hands to cover her face. It was as if in her need to make Andy understand her situation, she had finally realized the true consequences of her decisions herself. She seemed barely aware of Andy leading her to the couch and taking her into strong arms.

"Shhh," she said softly, rocking Brooke lightly and stroking her hair, her own heart beating rapidly as she felt Brooke struggle for breath.

"I'm sorry," Brooke finally managed, her head still pressed against Andy's chest.

"No, I'm the one who should be sorry," Andy said, her desire to calm down this obviously distraught woman overriding the instincts telling her this was a bad idea. For all she knew Brooke was some off-balance drama queen who was staging this scene so Jake would come to her rescue. "Of course you can stay here."

They remained close together in silence for a few more minutes before Brooke gently pushed herself away. "I'll make us some soup, if you're hungry," Andy offered. Brooke simply nodded and disappeared into the bathroom. Andy put her viola away in the music room, feeling even that space changed by Brooke's presence.

Her sanctuary had been invaded, and she knew without a doubt that things wouldn't be the same with Brooke in her life.

❖

She hadn't realized just how prophetic her worries were until she came into the living room to check on Brooke before she went to sleep. Brooke lay on the opened sofa bed with a book, wearing a red lace negligee, with what looked to be the entire contents of her suitcases strewn on the floor. She looked up as Andy entered the room, smiling faintly for the first time since she had entered the apartment.

"I didn't hear the explosion," Andy said, torn between staring at the mess or at the lovely woman in the see-through nightgown. The nightie was winning the battle, and she hoped her face wasn't as red as the satin and lace that barely covered Brooke's ample breasts.

"I am a bit of a slob," Brooke admitted unnecessarily. "But it only looks this bad because your apartment is obsessively neat."

"Yeah, that's it," Andy rolled her eyes. "I suppose that explains the state of my bathroom as well."

"I don't know how you can survive with only shampoo and moisturizer, but I'm thankful," Brooke said with a small grin. "Otherwise there wouldn't have been enough room for my things." Andy realized with some dismay that the woman seemed to have settled right in and made herself at home. Once the hurdle of getting through the door had been overcome, the apartment seemed to be *hers*, filled with her stuff, her presence, her smell.

"Can you come and sit with me?" Brooke asked, tentatively patting the bed next to her.

"Um," Andy hesitated, "is that what you're wearing to bed?"

Brooke looked down at her body as if she had forgotten what she had on. "All I have is the stuff I packed for my honeymoon in Barbados." She met Andy's gaze, her eyes narrowing. "I thought only guys were turned on by this sort of thing."

"They are," Andy lied, walking into her bedroom and returning with an old blue robe. "But put this on. I don't want you getting

cold," her eyes ran quickly over Brooke's body. "Or should I say
colder."

Brooke blushed and slipped her arms into the robe. Andy sat
gingerly on the bed next to her and decided she really hadn't helped
the situation much. Brooke wearing *her* bathrobe was definitely
as sexy as Brooke in lingerie. They leaned against the back of the
couch and regarded each other warily.

"Have you always known?"

"That I'm a lesbian?" Andy offered. At Brooke's nod she
continued. "At first I only noticed an absence of interest in boys
and dating. I thought it was because my parents fought so much that
I just didn't want any part of having a relationship." She avoided
Brooke's questioning gaze, not wanting to go into detail about her
family right now. "It wasn't until college that I realized it wasn't a
lack of emotion I felt, but that I hadn't found the right outlet for my
feelings."

"Who was she?" Brooke asked, feeling a surprising twinge of
jealousy toward this unknown woman from Andy's past.

"Carol. She played the clarinet," Andy answered. She glanced
at Brooke out of the corner of her eye and smiled. "Let's just say I
learned to appreciate the soundproof practice rooms in the music
hall."

Brooke laughed, and Andy asked her the same question. "What
about you? Are you going to tell me that until last week you had no
idea you might be a...might be a..."

Brooke pushed Andy's shoulder playfully. "Don't make fun of
me," she said.

"Why would I?" Andy asked, an innocent expression on her
face. "Just because you can do the deed, but you can't say the
word?" Brooke blushed at the memory, and Andy decided to let her
off the hook. "I do understand. What we did felt so right, so natural.
But it can be hard to accept the label and what it means in your life."

Brooke nodded, her eyes on the robe's sash that she pleated
with nervous fingers. "It was college for me, too," she admitted.
"I had been dating Jake since junior high. My parents never had
a touchy-feely sort of relationship, so I just assumed my lack of

passion for him was normal. They all decided I would join him at the University of Washington—he's a couple years ahead of me—and we'd get married as soon as he had his law degree, but I wanted to go to Gonzaga in Spokane instead of UW. It caused quite a scandal in my family," Brooke said with a grin. "My parents were so upset you'd have thought I told them I wanted to move to South America and be a drug runner and not simply go to a good private college a few hours away."

"Did they stage a high society intervention?"

"Practically," Brooke laughed. "But I insisted, and eventually they gave in." She shook her head, her expression quickly growing sad. "All of the effort to get my way wore me out, though. I fought so hard to go there, I started to question whether I really wanted it. It's crazy, but I was really homesick my first semester. Whenever I called home, I would hear about what a bad choice I was making and how Jake was surrounded by pretty girls at the U, so I never could admit I was lonely or that anything was less than perfect. I just got very…sad."

Andy reached over and hooked her index finger over Brooke's, tugging Brooke's hand onto her lap and holding it between both of her own. Brooke sighed and stared at their joined hands, finding it easier to talk about all of this without needing to look directly at Andy.

"The best part of college was my roommate Jan," she continued. "She's the one I stayed with this weekend. I knew she was gay from the start, she was very open about it and wanted me to have a chance to find a new room if I thought it'd be awkward. But it wasn't. Maybe because she talked about it so easily, or maybe because I felt drawn to her, I don't know. I asked a lot of questions, and she was always willing to answer them."

"Were the two of you…" Andy didn't want to finish the question. She realized she didn't want to hear that Brooke had been in her old lover's arms last night.

Brooke shook her head, and silky strands of hair brushed her shoulders, a light floral scent floating toward Andy. *Of course her hair smells good after using all of that crap littering the bathroom,* she told herself sternly, trying to stop her growing awareness of the woman next to her. Brooke continued. "She asked me out once, but I said no, that I wasn't a lesbian. She just laughed and said, 'Someday.'"

"And that someday happened?" Andy asked, continuing to draw the story from a reluctant Brooke.

"My RA noticed I was sad a lot, so she seemed to take an interest in me. I guess I misinterpreted what she meant, I mean, she was just trying to make me feel happier at school, and I developed a crush on her. It got so bad that she was all I could think about, fantasize about. She gave me a kiss good night once, just a friendly kiss like a sister, but I thought we were finally moving toward the relationship I wanted. I spent hours trying to work up the nerve to go to her, and when I finally did I found her in bed with one of the RAs from the guys' section of the dorm."

Brooke paused, but Andy kept silent, sensing the story wasn't over yet. She simply held her hand, trying to offer her support as she relived an obviously distressing experience.

"I started screaming at her," Brooke said with a small laugh, still embarrassed by the whole mess, but finding that Andy's comforting presence was easing her pain. In fact, with Andy so close on the bed, it was hard for Brooke to even remember her RA's face. "I caused quite a scene. My mother would have swooned. Liz, the RA, told me I was crazy and to get out. The next day she filed a complaint with the school. She told everyone in the dorm I was some obsessed stalker. It was humiliating. Jan was the only one who stood by me, she wanted me to stay at Gonzaga, said we could get an apartment and move out of the dorms. But I couldn't handle the way everyone looked at me, so I called home."

"Did you tell your parents everything?"

"Yes," Brooke said in barely a whisper. "About being homesick, about Jan…and Liz. They were convinced Jan had somehow corrupted me and put ideas in my head. They took me home and sent me to a therapist. I saw him for a couple of years."

"What did he tell you?" Andy asked, her voice hardening. She had a feeling she knew exactly what the therapist hired by Brooke's parents had said.

"That I was acting out my repressed anger toward my parents by choosing Gonzaga instead of UW and by imagining I wanted a relationship with another woman. He said I chose a straight woman to pretend to love because I didn't really want her to reciprocate."

"Do you believe that?" Andy asked. Brooke shrugged and she pressed on. "If she had been alone that night and had said she wanted you, would you have run away?"

Brooke paused and then gently shook her head. "I would have willingly been in her bed," she admitted. "I wanted her, and I was stupid enough to think she wanted me too."

"I don't know about that," Andy said thoughtfully. Things weren't adding up in her mind. Brooke didn't seem to be a woman who had trouble recognizing sexual attraction. "Are you sure she wasn't interested in you, but maybe scared of her own attraction to another woman? Didn't Jan believe you?"

"We've never really talked about her opinion of Liz, but like I said she already thought I was gay. She supported me, but I don't know if she thought I was misdirected with my feelings. Even though we've kept in touch over the years, she knows I won't talk about that night."

"Tell me more about how Liz acted around you," Andy prompted. The question caught Brooke off-guard, and she had to force herself to remember that semester. Every discussion since then, with her parents or her therapist, had focused on her own actions. After hours of painfully recounting the ways she had sought out Liz's company and the fantasies her inexperienced mind had created, Brooke wanted nothing more than to wipe the entire term from her memory. Everyone assumed Liz hadn't done anything to provoke her feelings, and Brooke had believed them. Andy was the first to question the situation from a new perspective, and Brooke expected to have little evidence to support her crush, so she was surprised by how many examples of Liz's attention came to mind.

"Well, she would touch me a lot," she said slowly. "Just on the shoulder or arm, you know, nothing sexual but very intimate. She always seemed to be in the showers when I was, and she'd come in my room to talk while I was changing. I felt like she was watching me, like she wanted me." Brooke spoke with growing assurance. Reliving these memories as an experienced woman and not as a lonely girl away from home for the first time helped her recall the subtle signs of interest Liz had shown, signs she had intuitively recognized but that everyone else had seemed determined to ignore. Andy's simple question about Liz had helped confirm Brooke's feelings almost as much as their night together had.

"Brooke," Andy said softly, leaning forward and making Brooke turn her head and meet her gaze. Their faces were so close they were almost touching. "Kiss me like she kissed you that night."

Brooke did. It was a brief kiss, with closed mouths, but definitely not chaste. Liz's kiss, even with the thrilling promise of making Brooke's schoolgirl daydreams come true, hadn't affected her nearly as much as the light brush of Andy's lips. One simple touch and Brooke's mind flooded with images from Thursday night, clearly conjuring up memories of every place Andy's lips had traveled. Brooke pulled back and looked at Andy with questioning eyes, hoping to see a reflection of the attraction she felt.

Andy sighed for Brooke. So many years of doubting herself and thinking she was crazy to believe what she did. "Do you ever kiss friends like that?" she asked. Brooke shook her head slightly. "Look, I can't say for certain because I wasn't there, but it sure sounds to me like this Liz wanted you. If she was afraid or confused by what she was feeling, then it would make sense that she might try to reaffirm her straightness by jumping in bed with some random guy. Especially after she made a move like kissing you."

"You really think so?" Brooke asked softly, facing forward again and dropping her head back onto the couch. She wrestled with the idea that she might have read all the signs correctly back then, and that Liz might have been just as attracted and panicked as she was. How different these past few years could have been if she had been able to see the experience through Andy's eyes. Or if she had met Andy instead of Liz…

Brooke disengaged the hand that Andy held and slid it along Andy's thigh, kneading slightly with her fingers. She heard Andy's sudden inhale and knew with pleasure that this woman wanted her.

"Careful," Andy breathed into her ear, her voice a caress. "I'm not some frightened coed, you know."

"I do seem to remember that you were very sure of yourself Thursday night," Brooke murmured, moving her hand farther up Andy's thigh.

"I remember some other things from that night," Andy said, nuzzling Brooke's neck. She ran her hand across Brooke's stomach, loving the feel of satin under her palm. "Liz was a fool."

Brooke reached up to cup her intimately, but Andy gently recaptured her hand and held it between both of her own, sitting up and putting some distance between them. Brooke's eyes were full of question and doubt, and Andy barely resisted the urge to just give in and kiss her.

"I'm not rejecting you," she said firmly, holding Brooke's gaze. "You know I want you, you can feel that I do. But you need time to think and make decisions. And I don't want to start a relationship that you're not prepared to follow through." Andy didn't add that after two painful days of missing Brooke, she couldn't allow herself to fall back into her arms only to be hurt again tomorrow.

Brooke's expression shut down again, whether in anger or humiliation Andy couldn't tell, and she rolled onto her side facing the far wall. Andy sighed and got off the bed, pulling the covers over Brooke and turning out the light. Her quiet good night went unanswered.

CHAPTER EIGHT

A ndy woke up just before dawn, after a restless night of tossing and sporadic sleep. She peeked into the living room and saw Brooke sprawled across the sofa bed, still wrapped in Andy's robe. She fought the temptation to wake her with a kiss, knowing exactly where that would lead, and instead made her way into the bathroom.

It took several minutes of searching through Brooke's clutter before she finally found her toothbrush. She roughly brushed her teeth, berating herself in the mirror the entire time.

It was one thing, she told herself, to offer a place of refuge to this woman who obviously needed somewhere to stay and think things through. And Andy reluctantly admitted that she had some responsibility for Brooke's confusion since she had taken her, an engaged woman, to bed that night. *So fine,* she told her reflection, *you let her in your home and you help her find a job. You listen when she needs to talk about her conflicting feelings or a difficult past. You even comfort her when she is sad or anxious. But you do not,* and here Andy stopped brushing and leaned toward the mirror, *I repeat, do* not *make matters more confusing by lying in bed next to her and kissing her.*

Andy glowered at herself a few moments longer, ashamed and angry that she had almost taken advantage of Brooke's vulnerability last night. *Remember,* she jabbed a finger at her reflection, *she is here to sort through a messy situation, not to be your plaything.*

Andy continued her lecture in the shower until she found herself hoping Brooke would wake up and come looking for her. She pictured wet blond hair, soapy lather cascading over those full breasts, Brooke's moans as Andy's fingers found her…

"Christ," Andy muttered, flipping off the hot water in an angry motion to see if an icy cold shower really would cool her passion. At least it was miserable enough to make her hurry out of the tub and into her clothes. She was leaning against the kitchen counter, eating a bowl of cereal and looking somewhat composed, when Brooke finally crawled out of bed.

"Coffee?" she croaked, her honey-colored hair tousled and her eyes only half-open.

Not a morning person, Andy decided silently as she handed Brooke a mug of coffee. She brought out the sugar in response to another mumbled request and didn't hide her grimace as Brooke shoveled several spoonfuls into her cup.

"Cream?"

Andy had to laugh when Brooke looked from the carton of soy milk to Andy's face with a horrified expression. "You expect me to put *this* in my coffee?" she asked in disbelief.

"It's soy milk, not a dead rat," Andy said, shaking the carton and setting it on the counter. "I'm a vegetarian and I don't eat dairy. Besides, with all that sugar, how will you know the difference?"

"I'll know," Brooke muttered, but she apparently decided she had no choice and added the milk to her mug. She took a small sip and sniffed. "I guess it'll do," she said as she disappeared into the bathroom.

"Good morning to you, too," Andy said to the closed door as she replaced the milk in the fridge and washed her cereal bowl. She heard the shower running and, in an effort to keep from sneaking into the bathroom, she headed to her music room for morning practice.

❖

Andy's mind wandered toward a showering Brooke for the first fifteen minutes of her practice while her fingers ran through the scales she knew so well. But as she moved through her routine, her mind regained its focus, and the rest of the world, including a distracting blonde, faded into nothingness. She started with her quartet work, including a love song from the latest Disney cartoon they knew would become popular with brides. Then she spent an hour on the Dvořák symphony for Wednesday night's concert before tackling the Clarke sonata. She worked slowly through the first movement, stopping occasionally to make notes in the score's margins. After she identified all of the potential trouble spots, she played it again at tempo, enjoying the contrast of the viola's deep voice and the lively rhythm of the movement. Clarke had written the sonata in 1919, when women composers were uncommon and often unrecognized. As Andy played she started to realize what it meant that she was able to hold the first viola chair and perform this piece, helping to introduce her audience to one of the women who had paved the road of her career. She found herself caught up in the music, and it wasn't until she was wiping excess rosin off the strings of her instrument with a soft cloth that she noticed Brooke leaning in the doorway.

"Hey, you look more awake," she said, her smile restored by the music.

Brooke pushed off the doorjamb and entered the room. She was careful to hide the rush of emotion she felt while watching Andy play. Her obvious love of the music showed clearly on her face, her full lips softening in a slight smile. With her arms raised to hold the instrument and bow, her shirt lifted enough to reveal a smooth, tight stomach with just a hint of white briefs peeking over the waistband of her loose-fitting sweatpants. Brooke swallowed and reluctantly moved her gaze back to Andy's face. "I need my coffee in the morning," she said as Andy finished cleaning her viola.

"I noticed," Andy said wryly. She handed the instrument to Brooke, who hesitated before taking it.

"It's beautiful," she said, running her hands lightly over the curved edges and worn varnish of the viola. She held the neck of the instrument where the satiny wood was still warm from Andy's palm. It was a poor substitute for Andy's direct touch, but Brooke didn't want to push for more right now. She had a feeling her presence in this room, the invitation to share a little in Andy's world of music, was almost as intimate a gesture for her as taking Brooke to bed had been.

"She is," Andy agreed. "Do you play an instrument?"

Brooke shrugged. "I took piano lessons when I was younger, but nothing serious. Nothing like how you play," she added, almost shyly.

"That's just a lot of years of practice," Andy said.

"No, there's more than that." Brooke shook her head. "The way you looked when you were playing, especially that last piece. It transforms you."

"Music can have that power over most people, if they let it."

Brooke handed the viola back to Andy. "I heard you play at the church of course," she continued, wincing slightly at the mention of her rehearsal. "But not a real song like this one," she gestured at the music on Andy's stand.

"As a violist, I mostly play the harmony and other instruments have the melody line. This was written by a viola player named Rebecca Clarke, and it's pretty rare to find a piece written to showcase my instrument."

"Why did you choose the viola?" Brooke asked.

"I started on the violin, but my high school music teacher asked me to try his viola because we needed one in the orchestra. He also thought it would help me get a scholarship since there tend to be fewer violists than violinists trying for college spots, and I had to pay my own way through school. I tried it once, and I was hooked," she said. "At first it felt awkward just to hold the viola because it was so much bulkier than my violin, but once I heard its voice, I knew it would be worth the extra effort to play. It's more physical than the violin, I guess, less fragile-feeling to me. It takes more strength to make a good tone, but once you learn how, the music just feels and sounds so much deeper."

Andy paused as if unable to find the right words. "Here, hold her like this," she said, positioning the viola on Brooke's left shoulder with her hand underneath to support it. Brooke tried to focus on her voice, but her attention faltered when Andy stepped behind her, and she could feel the warmth of Andy's body along her spine, the softness of Andy's breasts as they pressed into her back.

"This is the C string," Andy said, her hips shifting against Brooke's as she reached around her from behind and pointed to the thick string on the far left.

"There's not going to be a test on this, is there?" Brooke asked as she concentrated on not dropping the viola.

"Of course not," Andy said. "Just watch the string while I play C an octave higher."

Andy dropped the tip of her third finger onto the next string over and brought her right arm around Brooke so she could pull the bow across that string. As she played the fingered note, the open C string vibrated in response, and the whole instrument resonated under Brooke's chin.

"Wow," Brooke whispered as the note died away. "You can feel it through your whole body."

"Amazing, isn't it?" Andy smiled then returned the viola and bow to their case.

Andy turned to face her, and Brooke felt an awkwardness settle over them as the conversation came to a close.

"Come in here," Andy said as she took Brooke's hand and led her to the dining room where they sat at the small table.

"I just thought we should set some ground rules here," she began hesitantly. "You're probably feeling vulnerable now, and I think it would only muddle things if we were to sleep together."

"So, no sex is rule one?" Brooke asked.

"Exactly," Andy said, sounding relieved they were handling this well. "And nothing that might lead up to sex, like kissing."

"Or touching?" Brooke offered.

"Or holding hands."

"Or talking about sex."

Andy nodded, and then paused briefly. "And we need to find you something else to wear to bed."

"I told you I only have my honeymoon clothes," Brooke said, slightly irritated. "You have a lot of rules."

"I'm just trying to protect you and keep us from making a mistake. You can have one of my T-shirts."

"Then no tank tops without bras like you had on last night," Brooke said.

"I am not wearing a bra to bed," Andy informed her, crossing her arms over her braless chest.

"Fine," Brooke snapped. "Take it off when you're in your bedroom."

"Your grating personality will certainly help the no-sex rule," Andy muttered, trying to hide a smile.

"Thank you," Brooke said haughtily. "And your compulsive neatness makes you particularly unappealing."

Andy laughed. "Good, at least we agree on something. We're both too obnoxious to be sexy."

Brooke leaned her elbow on the table and propped her head on her hand. "Although we didn't seem to mind each other's flaws on Thursday," she said with a grin.

Andy counted on her fingers silently. "You just broke rule five, I think," she said. She glanced at the clock and groaned. "I have lessons to teach, and I really need to get going. Will you be all right today?"

"I'll be okay, don't worry," Brooke said, hiding her dismay at having a whole day to spend alone, dwelling on her problems. "You teach the viola? I thought you just did the symphony and weddings."

"None of them pays enough on its own," Andy shrugged. "Most musicians either have regular jobs as well, or they do anything musical that comes along, like I do. I teach a couple of days a week." She got up from the table and wrote a number on a notepad hanging on the fridge. "I'll be home a little after five. Here's my cell number. Call if you need anything."

Brooke nodded. "I'll be okay," she repeated, trying to reassure both of them.

Andy looked at her closely, as if reluctant to leave. "We can talk more when I get back," she said. "I know you have a lot of decisions to make, and I'll do what I can to help." With that she left, heading into her bedroom to change for work.

CHAPTER NINE

O nce she was alone, Brooke made an attempt to clean up some of the mess she knew bothered Andy. Deciding whether to cancel the wedding had consumed the past few days, but now that the choice had been made, Brooke faced countless new challenges. Straightening the apartment was more manageable than facing her mess of a life. She made up the sofa bed and folded it back, and then she stuffed most of her clothes into her suitcases and pushed them into a corner. Without more storage space, there was no way she could improve the bathroom situation, so she simply shut the door to hide the clutter.

Once she finished, she sat on the couch with Andy's old bathrobe clutched in her lap like a security blanket. Looking around, it was obvious to see she didn't belong in this place. Even after her efforts, anyone could tell there was an alien presence that had imposed itself on the apartment. Andy's belongings, her life, were ordered and tidy, while everything about Brooke spoke of confusion and chaos. For some reason, she hadn't been able to fit the clothes she took out of her suitcases last night back into them this morning, so some of her shorts and tanks were piled on top of them. A disorganized pile of summer sandals had been unsuccessfully hidden behind the cases. Except for one pair of jeans, she didn't have any clothes suitable for a Seattle autumn. She had been so distracted when she packed for her honeymoon she couldn't remember what she had with her, so last night when she had been desperately searching for something less revealing to wear to bed, she had emptied both cases. She had wanted to reassure Andy that she didn't usually fling all of her shit on the floor, but she'd been too embarrassed to tell her why she had displaced everything.

The scattered summer clothes might upset Andy's orderly nature, but to Brooke they were uncomfortable evidence of her aborted honeymoon. In the light of day, alone in the quiet apartment, Brooke faced the full impact of the choices she had made. She had been completely focused on running away from Jake and her old life, and she had spared little thought about where she was running *to*. She needed to find a job, even though she had few qualifications and no idea what kind of career she wanted. And while her bank account might cover a few weeks in a hotel, it couldn't possibly stretch enough to pay for an apartment of her own. Brooke knew her parents would help if asked, but returning to them for money seemed like a big step backward. If they were supporting her, they would expect to have some say in the decisions Brooke was finally ready to make on her own. She hadn't thought through the financial side of her escape, and she knew she couldn't rely on Andy's goodwill to keep her rent-free for long.

At the thought of Andy, Brooke pulled the robe a little tighter against her chest. She had come here wanting sex, wanting to lose herself in Andy's strong, confident embrace if only for a short time. She had hoped a repeat of Thursday night would give her the validation she craved, the assurance that the decision to leave Jake was the right one.

But Andy didn't want a brief sexual encounter. She had offered friendship instead, and her gentle exploration of Brooke's experiences in college gave Brooke a growing confidence in her own judgment, a confidence that had been badly shaken over the past few years. Brooke had thought of Andy as a gorgeous lesbian, someone who could make her feel good and give her a taste of real passion. But her short time in Andy's apartment had given Brooke a glimpse of Andy as a real person, not simply a sex partner. Her compassion and focus and independence attracted Brooke more deeply than she had anticipated, but they also scared her. For years, she had been too willing to let strong people control her, and she desperately wanted to protect the fragile possibilities of her new life. Already Brooke could sense Andy had higher expectations of Brooke than she had for herself. To help her find a job, accept her sexuality, stand on her own two feet. To help her make permanent changes when all Brooke had been looking for was a respite from the weariness of life. She couldn't live up to those expectations, couldn't match Andy's drive and talent and confidence, until she grew more sure of herself. The woman was too damned competent, and Brooke knew she looked like a spoiled child in comparison. She wanted to grow up, but she wanted to do it on her own terms— not Andy's or anyone else's.

Brooke rose finally and went into Andy's bedroom. She looked around this room that held no sign of her own presence, except in her memory. In her mind she could see the tangled sheets, smell their mingled aromas, taste her first experience with another woman. But in reality, there was only space for Andy in this tidy, sparse room. She quickly crossed to the closet and hung up the bathrobe before borrowing a sweater. She held it to her face, filling herself with Andy's fresh, soapy smell before pulling it over her light summer top. She needed to get out of this place, take a walk in the open air, and then come back and get her things. Andy wasn't Jake or her parents, she wasn't trying to take over Brooke's life, but Brooke didn't trust herself to resist her strength. She wasn't going to trade one cage for another. She took the key Andy had left, locked the apartment door behind her, and knew that by the time Andy returned, she would be long gone.

Brooke wandered down Tenth Avenue to the commercial district on Broadway and found a small café without any difficulty. She ordered a nonfat latte and sat at a window table. The Capitol Hill area was so different from her normal downtown haunts that she felt like she was in a different city altogether. This really was a good place for her to hide out, she mused as she stirred several packets of raw sugar into her drink. There was little chance of being spotted by any of her parents' friends in this eclectic neighborhood.

She took a sip, almost moaning with delight at the taste of sweet, milky espresso, and watched the world walk past her window. The district Andy lived in was a magnet for Seattle's gay and lesbian community, but Brooke was surprised at the sheer diversity of people she saw. All ages and types were represented, and she relished the thought of the anonymity such an area afforded her. She could start over, be anyone she wanted, in a place like this.

Brooke finished her coffee and slowly wandered down the street, window-shopping and relaxing more and more as she walked. The streets were perfumed by the various ethnic restaurants that were getting ready for the lunch crowds. She was so accustomed to the upscale chains that made up a lot of downtown's shopping district that the number of unique eateries and stores was refreshing. She found a vintage-clothing shop and went inside to look for a small thank-you gift for Andy. She could leave the present with her good-bye note.

The sales clerk, a girl who appeared a few years younger than Brooke with long black hair and blunt-cut bangs, smiled at her from behind the counter when she entered the shop. Brooke returned the smile and then busied herself among the racks. She didn't see anything that looked right for Andy, but she pulled out a silky blue shirt and held it up to herself in the mirror.

"That's a beautiful color for you," the clerk said, coming to stand behind Brooke. "It makes your eyes look so blue they're almost clear."

"You're sure? I've been told they look too cold when I wear this color," Brooke said, tilting her head to one side as she regarded her reflection. She had tried on a dress this color for a party at the law firm, only to change at the last minute because Jake said it made her eyes look icy. He hadn't meant it as an insult, but she had been particularly sensitive to the adjective since he had used it occasionally in the bedroom. It wasn't one of the words Andy had used to describe her, Brooke thought with a smile.

"Whoever said that is crazy," the girl said with another smile, holding Brooke's gaze in the mirror. "You look anything but cold to me."

Jesus, she's flirting with me, Brooke thought in amazement. In all her life she had never had another woman, except Jan, make any sort of move toward her, and now after just one night with Andy she looked like a lesbian? She stared more closely at herself in the mirror and wondered what had changed. Whatever it was, it felt good, she thought, surprising herself with the realization. It was like she was being seen as herself for the first time, and she grinned broadly at the clerk.

"If you think it looks good, then I'll take it," she said. *Nothing wrong with a little flirting in return.*

The clerk took the shirt from her and led her back to the counter. "These would be perfect for you," she said, pulling a pair of sapphire-blue earrings out of the front case. The costume jewels were dangling in a setting of black filigree, and Brooke knew Jake would hate them. *I'll buy you some real sapphires, not those cheap paste ones,* he would have said.

"They're lovely," Brooke said. "I'll take them too."

The clerk started to ring up the purchases when Brooke noticed a tattoo of a rose on her wrist. She reached out to touch it gently.

"That's pretty," she said. "I've always wanted a tattoo."

"You should get one!" the girl encouraged, making no move to pull her hand away. "Imprints is just two doors down. They're real artists there."

"Oh, I couldn't," Brooke said nervously. "Did it hurt?"

"A little, of course," the girl answered. "But it's worth the pain."

Brooke thought about that as she took her change and bag. She was about to leave when the girl stopped her.

"You live around here?" she asked, her voice casual.

"I'm staying with a friend nearby…for a while."

"Well, stop in again sometime. It was nice to talk with you."

"You too, and I will," Brooke said, feeling like a different person than the one she had been just last week. As if to drive that idea home, she found herself standing in front of Imprints a moment later, staring at the sample pictures in the window and trying to ignore the large sign that said: Walk-ins Welcome. She and Jan had been planning to get tattoos together when they were at Gonzaga. Brooke had gone home, but Jan now had a dove on her right shoulder. That was for the best, she told herself. She could be rebellious with earrings, but not with a permanent tattoo.

She stopped then and questioned what she had been saying to herself. Was she really being rebellious buying those earrings? No, she liked the look of them, the way they matched the blouse, the way the salesgirl had picked them for her. It was as if every decision had to pass through a filter created by her parents and Jake.

Well, not this one, she thought, and pushed into the shop before she could falter in her determination.

"Hey, there," a scraggly young man welcomed her as she approached the front desk. A couple of other people were in the process of getting tattoos, and neither was screaming in pain, so Brooke pushed on.

"Hi," Brooke answered, stopping about halfway across the shop. "I was thinking of getting a little tattoo on my ankle, but if I need an appointment I can come back some other time," she added, half hoping he'd tell her to come back.

"Cool, I can do an ankle tat now, no problem," the kid answered.

Crap, thought Brooke.

"Do you have an idea, or do you want to look through the books?"

"I'm not sure. Do you mind if I look?" Brooke asked. The book of sample tattoos was huge and seemed like a good way to stall for time.

Brooke stepped forward and opened the book while the young guy hovered near her. *He probably smells my fear,* Brooke thought, *and he doesn't want to go far in case I try to run.* She flipped quickly past pages of skulls and bloody daggers, flowers and rainbows, not sure exactly what she wanted. How could she choose a symbol to represent herself if she was just discovering who she was? She stopped on a page filled with animal images, and an old memory resurfaced. Maybe it wasn't a matter of reinventing herself, she decided, so much as remembering who she used to be before she handed control of her life to other people.

"That one," she said, pointing.

"No problem," the kid said, filling out a form and handing it to Brooke. She signed the consent form without reading it, not wanting to hear about the things that could go wrong. Her foot would probably rot off, and her lawyer father would say she had it coming for signing without knowing all the facts.

Brooke followed him back and took off her sock and shoe while he gathered his supplies.

"I've never had a tattoo before," she told him, relieved she had at least shaved her legs that morning.

"I kind of figured," he answered, cleaning off her ankle.

Well, if she was looking for reassurance and coddling, she wasn't getting it from this kid, Brooke decided. She gritted her teeth and told herself it would be okay. Just get past the first jab, and the rest would be easy.

Brooke walked the short distance to a grocery store, wanting to stop random people on the street and show them her new tattoo. But she was under strict orders from Teddy, her tattoo artist, to keep her bandage on for two hours, so she would have to wait. Since she still didn't have a present for Andy, she decided to just buy a new carton of soy milk to replace the near-empty one she had used that morning. It wasn't much of a gift, but it was something.

She wandered through the health food section of the store, limping slightly only because her ankle felt strange, and found herself distracted by all of the frozen vegetarian items that were available. She picked up a package of fake chorizo and remembered a dish she and Jake had eaten in a Spanish restaurant a few weeks ago. That was an idea. She could make dinner and leave it in the fridge for Andy tonight. She put the sausage in her basket and added several more ingredients from the produce aisle. While she selected a bag of frozen artichoke hearts, she decided that as long as she was cooking it might be okay to stay just one more night. That way they could eat together, and she would have someone to admire her tattoo. Brooke couldn't remember when she had last spent time on her own, doing exactly what she wanted to do, and she smiled at the thought of sharing her afternoon's activities and revelations with Andy. Tomorrow was soon enough to face the realities of her new independence, and she didn't want to end the day in a lonely hotel room, eating takeout by herself. One more night wouldn't hurt, would it?

❖

Andy unlocked her apartment door, resigned to the idea that Brooke had most likely returned home. She had spent most of the day, while her students struggled through their scales and simple pieces, convincing herself that both of them would be better off away from each other. She was startled by the rush of relief she felt when she saw Brooke's suitcases in her living room. Even more surprising was the almost-tidy state of what had been a disaster area just this morning.

Brooke appeared out of the kitchen, smiling shyly at Andy, who couldn't hide her own welcoming grin. "Something smells great," she said.

"It's paella," Brooke answered. "Vegetarian, of course."

Andy went into her music room to put away her teaching supplies and to take a moment to catch her breath. *Don't get used to it,* she warned herself. *Don't get used to coming home to warmth and thoughtfulness and* her. The sight of Brooke stirred her insides more than the appetizing smell stirred her empty stomach. But Andy knew the familiarity and comfort of Brooke's old life would soon call her back, and she needed to keep her distance so she could survive being alone again.

"Whoa," Andy said when she entered the small kitchen.

Brooke followed Andy's eyes as they swept over the counters. "Okay, I know I made a bit of a mess, but don't worry. I'll clean up after dinner."

Brooke's bit of a mess apparently included every pot and pan that Andy owned. "No," she said, swallowing her desire to immediately start cleaning. "You cooked, so I'll do the dishes." She peered into a pan that was coated with cooked rice. "Although it may take me all night."

Brooke swatted her with a towel. "It's not that bad. Now come eat."

They sat at the small dining room table, and Andy dished up the paella while Brooke opened the Spanish wine she had bought to go with the meal.

"God, that's amazing," Andy sighed, closing her eyes in rapture as she chewed her first bite. "Where'd you get the recipe?"

"I just tried to copy a dish that we...that I had in a restaurant once. I added tarragon, which is different from what I had there, but I like it."

"Well, it's worth every hour I'll be in there scrubbing pans."

Brooke rolled her eyes and took a sip of her red wine. "Now ask me what else I did today," she said.

"What else did you do today?" Andy asked obediently.

Brooke pulled up the leg of her jeans and showed Andy her ankle. It was slightly puffy and red, but the small tattoo was clearly visible.

"A tiger," Andy said, lifting Brooke's bare foot onto her lap so she could see it better. "I love it. What made you pick this design?"

"It was my nickname when I was little," Brooke confessed. "My dad used to call me his little tiger because I was strong willed and used to fight to get my way." Her voice softened and she dropped her gaze. "I don't really know when I changed, but I want to be that person again."

Andy brushed her thumb gently over the tattoo, still holding Brooke's foot in her lap. "I've seen plenty of tiger in you," she said.

"Really?" asked Brooke with a smile.

"Yes," Andy laughed, finally letting Brooke's foot go. "And I'm glad you think that's a compliment."

"Do you have one? A tattoo?" Brooke asked, taking another gulp of wine to hide the shiver that ran over her when Andy touched her sensitive skin. She fought the urge to crawl into Andy's lap where her foot had been cradled just moments ago.

"You don't remember?" Andy asked with a suggestive grin. Brooke swept her gaze over Andy as she tried to picture a tattoo somewhere on her body. Her mind easily conjured up clear images of Andy naked, and she hoped Andy would attribute her sudden flush to wine and spicy food.

Andy let her off the hook and turned in her chair, pulling her T-shirt up enough to reveal her lower back.

"Ooh," Brooke gasped a little. "How sexy!"

She ran her hands across the small viola that was etched along Andy's lower spine, flanked by two ribbons of music. Brooke was more mesmerized by the heat of Andy's skin than the tattoo itself, and she pulled her hands away abruptly. This physical attraction she felt would only make it harder for her to resist Andy's influence, her strength. She struggled to keep her voice steady. "Are the notes from a real song?"

"Mozart," Andy said, dropping her shirt and turning back to her food. "The first measures of 'Eine Kleine Nachtmusik.' I'm sad you forgot it so quickly."

"Stop teasing. I didn't see the back of you that night, and you know it," Brooke said, her thoughts turning to her one night in Andy's arms. Andy cleared her throat, letting Brooke know her thoughts were there as well. "I'm not ready for anything that elaborate yet," she said, twisting her ankle so she could admire it. "But I love my tiny tiger."

Andy reached out a hand and covered Brooke's. "It's meaningful and subtle. It's exactly right for you."

"By the way, do you realize you've broken rules three and five? You touched me, and you brought up sex."

Andy glanced behind her at the dirty kitchen. "Well, I know what my punishment is going to be. And by the time I'm finished I won't have the strength left to break rule number one."

CHAPTER TEN

A ndy came out of the shower the next morning to find Brooke huddled on the sofa bed with her cell phone cradled to her ear. *Jake,* Andy thought. *Damn.*

They had ended up doing dishes together the evening before, talking about how much Brooke disliked her job at the firm and laughing about her childhood ambitions of driving an ice cream truck or being a ballerina. They had been careful to avoid any physical contact with each other. Andy knew she wanted to protect her own feelings in case Brooke left, and to give Brooke time to adjust to this new life. She could only guess at the reasons behind Brooke's reluctance to touch her. Maybe she didn't want to encourage a relationship? Or had she realized her attraction to Andy had only been a way to escape a life of dependence? Andy preferred to think Brooke might be feeling the same way she was, and that any touch between them could ignite a passion they weren't yet ready for.

But the thought of Brooke leaving made her realize that although she wasn't ready now, she wanted the option to stay open. She wanted Brooke around, whether they were having sex or just becoming friends. Andy went into her music room, but she didn't immediately take out her viola, hoping Brooke would come talk to her after the phone call.

She had been learning a lot about this woman who had been a stranger, a client, to her only a week ago. Andy was starting to recognize that the cool, unemotional exterior that Brooke usually maintained was just a thin, protective shell around a warm, funny, perceptive woman. Most people only saw a distant, unreadable woman, like Andy had at first. But the occasional glimpses of sadness, humor, and stubborn determination were becoming more frequent as Brooke became more comfortable just being herself. And Andy had a growing desire to help Brooke. Not to dictate her life like others had, but to help her find work that filled her eyes with passion, to be there as she confronted the deep sadness that she carefully hid from the world, and to be in her arms as she explored the sexuality she had been denying so long. *Careful,* Andy cautioned herself, *someone might get the mistaken impression that you're falling in love.*

Brooke tapped lightly on the open door, startling Andy out of her reverie. "That was Jake," she said with all the emotion of someone announcing the couch was lumpy or it was time for dinner. Andy wasn't fooled by her apparent lack of emotion, but she was too afraid to ask if Brooke was leaving, so she remained silent.

"He's staying with a friend in Oregon since he already had the week off," Brooke continued. "I need to go to our place for more clothes, and I wanted to let him know. And to make sure he's okay."

Brooke's voice shook slightly, and she didn't resist when Andy pulled her into her arms. Brooke leaned into the hug, needing this woman's strength more than she cared to admit. The call had left her devastated. Jake had every reason to be furious with her, and she had been prepared for yelling and recriminations. Instead he had just sounded so sad and confused that she felt racked with guilt. She had strung him along for years, and she hated herself for hurting him in the search for her own happiness. But Jan had been right. She had wounded Jake by leaving, but how much worse if she subjected him to a lifetime in an unhappy marriage?

"Will you come with me?" Brooke asked, her voice muffled against Andy's shoulder. "I know it's your practice time…"

"That can wait," Andy assured her. "Of course I'll come."

❖

Brooke directed Andy to the high-rise apartment she shared with Jake. She hesitated by the open door as if reluctant to enter, so Andy gave her a slight push and closed the door behind them.

"How about a tour?" she asked, hoping to give Brooke a little time to reorient herself before they started packing. Brooke led her into the apartment that was easily twice the size of Andy's, and took her first to the large picture window in the living room. The view of Lake Union was spectacular, and Andy watched a seaplane land on the choppy water before she turned and slowly surveyed the room again.

"You live here?" she asked.

"Of course," Brooke said. "I thought you knew Jake and I were living together."

"I did," Andy hesitated before she tried to explain. "It just doesn't look like your place."

Brooke studied the living room. "Jake lived here before I moved in, so he had already decorated. I guess I didn't really add much."

Andy nodded, but she had meant more than simple home décor. In just a few days, Brooke had filled her apartment with a *presence* that invaded every room, not just the ones that were covered with her clutter. There were photos of Brooke and Jake scattered around this room but no feeling that she belonged here.

Brooke moved on to the kitchen. It was decorated with black granite and fixtures, and had a modern, unused feel to it. She looked around, as if seeing everything for the first time. "We don't cook much here," she said, running a hand along the bare countertop. "We mostly use the microwave, or we eat out with clients or other lawyers from the firm. Jake likes to socialize, and he thinks it's good for his career."

"But you like to cook," Andy said, remembering her delicious dinner from the night before.

Brooke shrugged. "I haven't done much since I was a child. Jan and I would bake cookies and things in the common room of our dorm, but my family has always eaten out a lot. Last night was for you."

Andy met her gaze and was about to move toward her when Brooke's attention was caught by something behind her. "That," she pointed, "is coming with us."

Andy laughed when she saw the fancy espresso machine tucked in the corner, under a cabinet. "I knew you didn't like my coffee."

"I was trying to be polite, but it's horrible."

"So you're being *polite* when you drink it and make that face?" Andy laughed.

"That's the best I can do in the morning. I'll start making you soy lattes with this baby, and you'll never go back." Brooke walked past her, bumping her with a shoulder and giving the espresso machine a pat as she left the kitchen. Andy smiled and followed, happy to feel Brooke's tension easing.

"This is one of the bathrooms, here's the guest bedroom, and Jake's den." Brooke moved down the hall, pointing out the rooms while Andy continued to look for any sign of her touch.

"And this is the master bedroom and bathroom," Brooke said when they entered the large room that was decorated in shades of gold and brown. It was beautiful, torn from the pages of a magazine, but not what Andy had expected from Brooke's home. She realized it was because everything matched. She could picture Brooke dragging home a flea-market lamp or an ugly, but comfy, sofa, but not this elegant furniture that had obviously come as a set. She peered in the bathroom and finally saw some signs of Brooke's existence. She shut the door and stood in front of it with her arms crossed.

Brooke laughed at her expression. "I only have my vacation things at your place," she said, gesturing at the door behind Andy. "I'm going to bring most of that with me today, so deal with it."

"You can't fit any more crap into my bathroom," Andy growled, refusing to move as a laughing Brooke tried to push her out of the way. She grabbed Brooke's arms and spun them both around so she had Brooke pinned against the bathroom door. "So deal with that."

Brooke made a soft sound in her throat and snaked her arms around Andy's neck. Andy dropped her head and nuzzled Brooke's shoulder and hair. "You smell so good as it is," she murmured. "You couldn't possibly need more stuff to wash with."

Brooke threaded her hands through Andy's hair and pulled her face up so their lips met. Their kiss held all of the emotions from the stressful past week, and it deepened quickly. Brooke pushed against Andy again, and this time she let herself be moved backward until they collapsed together on the king-sized bed. Andy's hands slid under Brooke's T-shirt to touch her breasts, rubbing the lace of her bra over sensitive nipples and making her gasp in pleasure.

"Do you have good memories in this bed?" Andy asked, her breath hot against Brooke's ear.

Brooke shook her head, blond hair trailing over Andy's face. "Not really," she admitted. "But I wouldn't mind making a few right now."

Andy flipped Brooke onto her back and slid her hand down between Brooke's thighs. She groaned when she felt a surge of warmth, knowing how wet Brooke would be to her touch. She was eagerly undoing the top button on her jeans, all of her resolutions to take things slow fading away, when they heard the front door open.

"Brooke? Are you here?" a male voice called.

"Shit!" Brooke hissed as they jumped off the bed. She tucked her shirt in and buttoned her jeans while Andy hastily straightened the bed covers.

"Is it Jake?" Andy asked, raking a hand through Brooke's tousled hair. Brooke shook her head.

"My parents were going to water the plants while we were gone. Damn, Jake must have called them," she whispered then raised her voice. "I'm in the bedroom, Daddy. Be right out."

"Maybe I should just tell them?" she asked, throwing an agonized look at Andy. They had started for the living room when Evelyn and Bill Stanton appeared in the bedroom doorway.

"Jake told us you'd be at the apartment, Brooke darling," her mother said, her eyes sliding over Andy and dismissing her. "He wanted us to come over and make sure you're okay."

"I'm fine, Mom. I just needed to get a few things."

Andy watched as Brooke's dad took in their untidy state and the lack of any sign of packing going on in the bedroom. His eyes locked with hers, and she knew not to underestimate him and his ability to interpret the situation. Every ounce of her wanted to move in front of Brooke like a shield and protect her, but she worried any indication of a relationship between her and his daughter would only make him angrier. She had to find a way to get Brooke out of this apartment.

"Let's take this into the living room," Bill growled. Evelyn seemed surprised at her husband's controlled anger as he glared at Andy.

"You're the woman from the quartet," she said slowly, finally placing Andy. "You came to the dressing room before the rehearsal, and…"

Her voice trailed away as she looked from Andy to her daughter. "Oh, Brooke, not this again!"

Brooke opened her mouth to speak, but Andy held up a hand to stop her. *Just get her out of here,* her mind yelled. *Don't let her say things she'll regret, things that will make her father even angrier.* "Brooke and I are just friends, Mrs. Stanton. She's staying with me while she figures things out."

Brooke's eyes met hers, her hurt expression quickly changing to a neutral one. "She's right, Mom. There's nothing between us." She turned back to face her parents, leaving Andy reeling as she felt Brooke's withdrawal from her like a physical thing. "Nothing."

Bill looked unconvinced, but Evelyn seemed all too happy to accept Brooke's statement. "Then there's no reason to stay away from Jake any longer, is there? We can drive you down to Oregon to see him. A little vacation will do you both good."

"No, Mom," Brooke said firmly. "I need time to think. Jake and I decided to separate until Christmas, and I'm taking that time."

"This is ridiculous," Bill said dismissively. "You're acting like a spoiled brat. If he did something to make you mad, you deal with it at home, not with some…stranger."

"I need my space," Brooke frowned.

"Then we'll get you a place," Evelyn offered. "Maybe in Bellevue or Tacoma. You and Jake can date while you work things out. That would be fun, wouldn't it?"

"No," Brooke shouted, startling all of them. "I don't want you supporting me, and I do not want to date Jake. I just need time to think."

"But it's fine for *her* to support you," Bill said in a clipped voice, waving his hand toward Andy, who winced slightly at the gesture.

"Andy's neutral," Brooke said, stepping forward and putting her hand on her dad's arm. "So I can be more objective at her place and figure out what I really want. I know you understand that since it's how you deal with difficult clients."

Andy didn't see how she was in any way neutral in this situation, but Brooke's words had their desired effect on her dad, and he covered her hand briefly with his own. Andy felt the tension in the room ease. "I didn't think you ever listened when I talked about business strategies," he said with a flicker of a smile. "It's not fair to throw that back at me."

Brooke shrugged, a small answering smile playing over her face. "I have to talk so you'll understand me."

Evelyn looked at her husband and daughter with some confusion. "So you're not going to make her come home?"

"She's an adult," he said to his wife with a resigned sigh. "I can't make her do anything."

"But we can't just leave her with…her," Evelyn looked at Andy with obvious distaste. Andy wasn't insulted by that. The potential danger of Bill Stanton's anger seemed to be gone, and all she felt was a sagging sense of relief.

"She and Jake decided to give it until Christmas, so we have to support that," he said, giving Brooke an awkward pat on the shoulder. "You'll at least let us know the number and address where you're staying?"

Andy gave her information to Bill, who recorded it on his cell phone, and then she stayed in the bedroom to give Brooke a few minutes to say good-bye to her parents.

"I was going to tell them," Brooke said coldly when she returned. Andy was sitting on the bed with her elbows on her knees and her head in her hands. She raised her head at Brooke's voice. "I was going to tell them about us, that I think I'm gay. But you said there was nothing between us."

Andy knew pain lurked behind the emotionless mask Brooke wore. "That's just it," she said sadly. "You *think* you're a lesbian. You *think* you might want a relationship with me. What if you change your mind? Why tell them things that will make them angry and hurt them if you're still not sure?"

"I guess you're right. After all, it's not like we have anything real between us."

Andy didn't answer. What she felt for Brooke was frighteningly real to her, but Brooke still wasn't sure who she was. She still held on to Jake, to that distant Christmas deadline, and Andy had to protect herself from the hurt she'd feel if Brooke left.

"I guess I'll get packed," Brooke said quietly.

"Then home to neutral Switzerland." Andy tried to joke but failed, and silence fell between them.

The uncomfortable silence lasted through the process of packing most of Brooke's belongings and taking them back to the apartment. Brooke had gained her dad's reluctant acceptance of her separation from Jake, and that victory was the only thing keeping her in Andy's life. She had convinced him that staying with Andy while she sorted out her feelings was a mature decision, and it would have seemed too flaky to tell her parents she had changed her mind yet again.

She didn't have to like it though. It took three trips to get everything into Andy's apartment, and the physical labor did nothing to cool Brooke's temper. She could see the concern on Andy's face every time they passed on the stairs, but Brooke was too angry to care. She had expected Andy to stand up for their relationship, not to betray it. She should have helped Brooke confront her parents so she could get on with life without all this secrecy.

"I'll let you get settled," Andy said, once all of Brooke's boxes were upstairs.

"Fine."

"I'll be right back. You won't leave, will you?"

"No."

Andy rolled her eyes and grabbed her car keys before she left the apartment.

Brooke started unpacking her clothes without pausing to wonder where she was going to put them. Her monosyllabic responses to Andy's attempts at conversation gave way to long muttered tirades once she had her privacy, and the combination of flinging clothes around the room and swearing eased Brooke's tension.

"How could she..." Brooke's voice faltered to a stop, and she sat on the sofa with a thump. Without Andy in the room as a target for Brooke's anger, its real object suddenly seemed clear. Yesterday, Brooke had been so concerned about asserting her independence, but the minute she was in a tense situation she had automatically looked for Andy to tell her parents what *Brooke* was feeling, what *Brooke* wanted. All of her big plans to seize her new life had fallen apart at the first sign of confrontation, and she'd hidden behind Andy like a mewling kitten.

Brooke reluctantly admitted to herself that Andy hadn't betrayed her. She had rightly left the decision to come out to her parents in Brooke's court. Although she had seemed almost desperate to calm everyone down, Andy never tried to take Brooke's control away from her. She did downplay their relationship, but whether or not they were lovers wasn't really the issue. Brooke needed to tell her parents how she was struggling with her own sexuality, but her relationship—or not—with Andy was none of their business. Brooke had the chance to be honest with her parents, and she had passed it up. At least she hadn't given in to their demands about Jake.

Brooke had expected her life to transform overnight, for every new step to be as easy as getting her tattoo, but apparently it took more than a little ink and pain to completely change a person. Brooke looked around with a sigh, finally noticing the mess she had created. She wondered if she had enough time to clean it up before Andy returned.

Brooke managed to get most of her clothes off the floor before Andy got back to the apartment. "I don't have any place to put my stuff," she said.

"It doesn't matter," Andy said with a shrug. "There's not much in the hall closet, so I'll clear that out for you. And we can get a dresser for your clothes. Later, though. Come out with me now."

"Where?" Brooke asked, reluctant to leave.

"On a picnic. It's cold out, so dress warm."

"Are you crazy?"

"All signs point in that direction," Andy said, putting on a scarf and jacket and grabbing a blanket. "Are you coming or not?"

Brooke picked up a jacket she had tossed on the sofa and pulled it over the heavy sweater she had borrowed from Andy that morning.

Andy drove them to Volunteer Park, parking by the Asian Art Museum. She got out of the car with the blanket and a bag of food from the deli.

"Can't we just eat in the car?" Brooke called out the window.

"No. There's a nice place to sit over here, so come on," Andy said as she started walking. Brooke trotted to catch up and followed Andy behind the museum and down a slope. They saw quite a few people running or biking along the road, but the grassy areas were almost empty because of the cold weather. Andy led them to a small area that was sheltered by trees, giving them a little privacy, and spread the blanket on the ground.

She sat down and started to unpack the bag. "Not much of a picnic, but it's the best I could do on short notice. We do a lot of weddings here, and Tina and I found this spot last summer."

Brooke stood stubbornly for a few moments before dropping to the blanket with a long-suffering sigh. She watched as Andy laid out bagels, a packet of cream cheese for Brooke, apples, a container of Kalamata olives, and a dark chocolate bar for dessert. Andy opened a couple of bottles of cream soda and handed one to Brooke.

"This is nice," Brooke said irritably.

Andy smiled. "It's impossible to stay mad at someone who takes you on a picnic."

"Not impossible," Brooke muttered. "But not very easy, damn you."

They ate quietly, but at least the silence seemed less strained and Andy looked more relaxed, leaning back against a large rock. She took a drink of her soda, watching as Brooke licked cream cheese off her fingers.

"I'm sorry I let things get out of control when we were at the apartment," Andy finally said.

"I was there too. I don't recall asking you to stop."

"No, but if your parents hadn't come in…"

"I know," Brooke said. "Tell me again why you're so against us having sex."

"I'm definitely for it," Andy admitted. "But we're in the first stages of a relationship. The sex is naturally exciting, and you don't want to base your decisions on that."

"So you don't believe this will last?" Brooke asked, gesturing between the two of them.

"It will last," Andy said quietly, "if it's what we really want. But you don't know yet, and it's hard to go slow when we're living together."

Even though Brooke agreed, in some part of her it hurt to think Andy might want her to leave. "So you think I should—"

Andy raised a hand to stop her. "No, I don't want you moving out. I kind of like having you around. But what you said to your dad made sense, and you should give yourself time to really consider your options. We just need to make an effort to keep control of the physical side of our relationship until you're clear about what you want."

"Well, I kind of like being around you, too," Brooke said grudgingly, unwrapping the candy bar and breaking off a piece for Andy while she tried to keep relief from showing on her face. "But I don't know where all of these high moral standards of yours were the night you took me to bed."

"Apparently they took a little vacation that night," Andy said with a laugh as she bit into her chocolate.

"They should get out more often," Brooke suggested. "But I'll admit you're right, and we should try to take this slowly. So I'll play things your way for now and stick with that stupid no-sex rule."

She shivered as a cold breeze swept across the grass. "Don't worry. I'm only coming over because I'm freezing," she said as she crawled over and curled up next to Andy, drawing the blanket around them and resting her head on Andy's shoulder.

"Well this certainly helps the situation," Andy muttered even as her hand caressed Brooke's back.

"Is it hard to always be the sensible one?" Brooke asked, snuggling closer.

"It sucks," Andy said. They sat together until the breeze grew into an uncomfortably chilly wind, forcing them to get up. Brooke packed up the remains of their lunch and tossed everything into the deli bag. As reluctant as she had been to come on this picnic, she hated to have it end. She wasn't accustomed to this sort of romantic gesture, one designed only to make her happy with no expectations to follow. *Jake would never have come up with a spontaneous, ridiculous idea like this,* Brooke thought before she pushed him out of her mind and started walking up the hill. Andy came up from behind and wrapped the blanket and her arms around Brooke, matching her steps as they made their way back to the car.

CHAPTER ELEVEN

An uneasy peace settled over Andy's apartment in the two weeks following their trip to Brooke and Jake's home. Andy resigned herself to the extra clutter, and Brooke's clothes now covered every bare surface in the living room. The bathroom was a lost cause, but Andy doggedly protected her music room, and anything of Brooke's that made its way in there was promptly removed and dropped on the sofa bed. The espresso machine was the one welcome addition, and after her first sip of the latte Brooke made with her special blend of coffee, Andy would have gladly given up her bed and slept on the floor if the machine had required it.

Andy could only watch as Brooke silently retreated into sadness while she struggled to build a new life. Her old job and once-active social life had been replaced by a fruitless career search and long hours spent alone in the apartment, and Andy was frustrated by her inability to help. She tried to make her home a sanctuary for Brooke, a place where she had the space she needed to work out the details of her life, but the effort to keep her at a distance was exhausting for Andy. Her self-control was tested daily as Brooke walked around half-dressed after her shower or lounged on the sofa bed wearing one of Andy's old T-shirts. Andy knew the struggle to hide her sexual frustration often made her sound irritable, so she spent more and more hours playing her viola in the apartment or in one of the practice rooms reserved for the symphony. At least her music benefited from the strained relationship with Brooke, and she was almost looking forward to the concert in December.

Brooke's one solace had become shopping for food and cooking, and Andy secretly looked forward to the days Brooke spent wandering through the local markets instead of job hunting. She would come home with bags of groceries and spend a few happy hours creating a meal for them to share. She disliked the confines of a recipe, and a few of her inventions had to be tossed in the trash, but Andy willingly took on the role of taster. On the nights when Brooke cooked, she would clear the career guides off the kitchen table, and they would eat together. For a couple of hours, Brooke would discuss spices and herbs while Andy felt the knots in her stomach slowly loosen.

Andy finished her practice one morning and left the music room, expecting to find an empty apartment since it was Brooke's usual shopping time. She was surprised then to hear voices coming from the living room and smothered a groan of despair when she found her sister sitting on a chair talking to Brooke.

"There you are," Brooke said with obvious relief, getting off the sofa and coming to greet Andy as if she had been gone for days. "Amy and I were having a chat while you practiced."

"Hey, Amy," Andy said and then spoke more quietly to Brooke. "You could have come to get me, you know."

Brooke shrugged. "I didn't want to interrupt. Can I get either of you something to drink?"

"Beer would be great, thanks," said Andy.

"Beer? But it's only…" Brooke started in surprise but stopped at Andy's meaningful look. "Sounds good. I think I'll have one also. Amy?"

"Why not?" Amy said with a laugh. "Alcohol always helps our family gatherings."

Andy sat on the couch facing her sister. The Goth look was sitting tiredly on the twenty-four year old, but Amy seemed determined to keep it up. It made their parents upset, and so it stayed.

"Well, why are you here?" she asked, hating the ungracious tone in her voice. "I mean, I haven't seen you in a couple of months."

"I know, and apparently you found yourself a new girlfriend since I saw you last," Amy said with an unattractive sneer on her face.

"I'm not her girlfriend," Brooke corrected as she returned with three beer bottles. She handed them around and dropped next to Andy on the sofa. "I'm just staying for a while."

"Cheaper than a flight to Geneva," Andy said and was rewarded with a smile and a jab from Brooke's elbow. They had taken to calling Andy's apartment Switzerland after Brooke's conversation with her dad, but Andy knew her true feelings for Brooke were anything but neutral.

Amy watched their small interchange and laughed. "Oh, please tell me you're bringing her to Thanksgiving dinner! I can't wait to see the folks' faces when the two of you show up."

"She is not coming to Thanksgiving with me," Andy said in a steely voice, not missing the flicker of pain that crossed Brooke's face.

"Chickenshit," Amy laughed.

"I'll make some sandwiches for lunch," Brooke offered quietly, getting up and collecting Andy's already empty beer bottle. Andy glared at her still-laughing sister and followed Brooke to the kitchen.

Brooke ignored her and reached into the fridge for another beer, but Andy grabbed her arm and forced her to turn and face her.

"Don't," she pleaded. "Don't think I'm ashamed of you or that I don't want to spend the holiday with you."

"Then why..." Brooke faltered as Andy's hand slid down her arm and along her waist, pulling her close. "Why are you so determined to make everyone think we're not, well, whatever we are?"

"Look, my family doesn't really accept that I'm a lesbian. It's just not something we talk about."

"What do you do, rent a guy for the holidays?"

Andy shook her head with a small laugh, not wanting to move away from the brief closeness she was feeling with Brooke. This was the first time they had touched since their picnic, and all she wanted to do was kiss her. But she had grown too accustomed to dealing with family issues on her own, not turning to anyone else for comfort or sympathy, so she reluctantly moved away.

"We just don't talk about it. As long as I never mention that I'm gay, we do all right. I wouldn't subject you to them."

Brooke reached out to touch Andy's arm, but Andy shied away from her hand and glanced at the kitchen door. "I was kind of hoping we'd spend the holiday together since I'd rather not go home. I know I'll be the main topic of conversation at our family dinner, so I already told Mom I have other plans. We could just tell your parents we're old friends or something."

Andy's face hardened. She had learned long ago to keep her friends, and later her girlfriends, far away from her family. "You don't understand. I will not take you there."

Amy walked in and set her empty beer bottle on the counter, looking at their faces. "Don't tell me the lovebirds are having a fight," she said with a playful frown. "I'd hate to break up a happy couple."

"No, you wouldn't," Andy said between gritted teeth as she grabbed two beers and herded Amy back toward the living room. She glanced back at Brooke who was watching her with one of those unreadable expressions. "You don't have to make food for us. She won't be staying long."

Brooke waved her away and quickly assembled ingredients for some simple sandwiches. Andy's behavior puzzled her. She seemed so sure of herself, but both with Brooke's parents and her own she was determined to hide any trace of their relationship. Brooke wouldn't discuss this in front of Amy since she so obviously rattled Andy, but as soon as she was gone, Brooke was going to get some answers.

She returned to the living room to find the two sisters stiffly talking about Amy's job at a local record store. She handed out plates of sandwiches and chips to the two women who seemed too different to be related. Amy was all harshness, from her overdone black and ghostly makeup to her bitter voice and words. Brooke wouldn't call Andy soft, but there was a kindness and sensitivity to her that seemed totally lacking in her sister. Her expressive eyes and hands betrayed a sensuality that she tried to hide for some reason, but Brooke knew it was there. She had seen it first hand when—

"What is this?" Amy's question jolted Brooke out of her dangerous line of thinking. Amy had lifted the top piece of bread and was picking at the contents of her sandwich.

"It's vegetarian lunchmeat," Brooke said, taking a bite of her own lunch. She was getting used to the taste of the stuff, especially when she disguised it with veggies and condiments.

"Oh, you're still on that trip?" Amy asked, picking at the sandwich until it was just tomato and stone-ground mustard. "Well, at least you'll get some turkey at Thanksgiving."

"What?" Brooke asked. Andy glared at her sister and waved off Brooke's question. "Tell me," she insisted. "What did she mean by that?"

"I usually eat a regular dinner at my parents' house," she said, avoiding eye contact with Brooke. "Just on the holidays."

"Anything to keep the peace, huh sister dear?" Amy said with a bitter laugh. She turned to Brooke. "I remember the first Thanksgiving that Andy tried to announce she was a vegetarian. You were in high school, weren't you?"

"Shut up, Amy," Andy said quietly, but with enough authority that Amy actually did as she said. There was a brief pause, then Andy asked about a couple of mutual friends, apparently a safe topic for the sisters since the uncomfortable conversation got them through lunch. Brooke took their plates to the kitchen while Andy shuffled her sister out of the apartment.

"Sorry about all of that," Andy said when she returned to the kitchen a few moments later. She picked up a towel and dried the dishes Brooke had washed. "She's a bit difficult to take."

"What happened at that Thanksgiving?" Brooke asked quietly, her eyes not leaving Andy's face as she put the plates in the cupboard.

Andy shrugged. "Dad yelled, Mom cried, the whole dinner ended up on the kitchen floor. Typical holiday at the Taylor house."

She grabbed another couple of beers from the fridge and led the way to the sofa.

Brooke sat next to her, one leg tucked under her hip. She took the beer that Andy offered and swallowed some while she worried how to phrase her next question.

"When we were with my parents, at Jake's house," she started, "my dad raised his hand toward you, and you flinched. Did you think he was going to hit you?"

"No," Andy said, gazing directly at Brooke. "I was scared he was going to hit *you*."

"Because your dad used to?"

Andy sighed and looked away, taking a long drink from her beer. "Not much. Nothing serious. Besides, I learned how to act, what to say, to keep things from getting out of hand."

"Like pretending that you're not a vegetarian lesbian?"

"Exactly," Andy said as she nervously picked at the label on her bottle. "I know that makes me a coward."

"No," Brooke said quietly. "I think it makes you very brave. To still be who you are even though you don't get approval for it."

"No. It's not brave to pretend to be someone else and to compromise my values. But the only other choice is to sit through the fights and to know that when I go home, I'm leaving my mother alone with him."

"Is this why you didn't want me to tell my parents about us?"

"I was afraid for you. I didn't know how they'd react."

Brooke frowned. "My father would never hurt me. No matter how angry he got."

"I didn't know that for sure. All I knew was that I wanted to protect you." Andy brushed the back of her hand along Brooke's cheekbone. Brooke sighed and leaned into the contact. She wanted to hold her, to wipe away the pain she had experienced in her past, but she worried Andy would shy away from any expression of sympathy. She had a feeling not many people were allowed to see beyond the controlled façade Andy showed the world, and for now it had to be enough that she had shared some of her past with Brooke.

They sat together, making no move to build on the light touch but each needing to feel close to the other. Finally Andy withdrew her hand.

"Let's get out of here," she said, draining the last of her beer in one long pull. "Do you want to go see a movie?"

"Are you asking me on a date?" Brooke asked.

"Huh, I guess I am," Andy answered, offering her hand to help Brooke up. "What do you think?"

"I think it's about time," Brooke said with a smile, giving Andy's hand a squeeze. "But it might be against the rules."

"To hell with the rules."

CHAPTER TWELVE

I'm not qualified to do anything," Brooke complained the next morning. Andy, her hair still wet from her shower, brought her coffee to the dining room table and glanced over Brooke's shoulder at the want ads she was reading. Brooke handed her a sheet of paper. "Look at this resume—it's only a half-page long, and Dad is my only reference."

Andy scanned the brief resume. "Maybe you could work as a paralegal at a different firm?"

Brooke knew Andy's suggestion was her most reasonable option, but much as she needed to find work, the thought of settling for some version of her old job made her feel like a failure. After her struggle to redefine herself and break free from the past, she hated to end up back where she started, not only doing work she disliked, but with the added risk of running into Jake at the courthouse on a regular basis. "It's the job they picked for me," she said quietly.

Andy tossed the resume back on the table. "Then take your time to find the right career for you," she said. "Don't settle. And in the meantime, I have a job you could do. It's just a one-time gig, though, and it only pays dinner at the restaurant of your choice."

Brooke looked up at Andy. "What exactly do you have in mind?"

Andy dropped into a chair. "No nudity required," she said with a laugh. "My students have their fall recital tonight. Pete, the other teacher, and I could use someone to organize things backstage. We usually have a parent do it, but they'd rather be out in the audience."

Brooke frowned. "Work with kids? I'm not sure."

"They won't give you any trouble. They'll all love you."

"I don't know about that, but if it'll help you, I guess I can do it."

"Perfect," Andy said, getting out of her chair and giving Brooke a quick kiss on the top of her head. "We should leave by four. Start thinking about where you want to eat after."

"For this I get sushi," Brooke announced, ignoring Andy's grimace and returning to her job search.

❖

"Your recital is in a church?" Brooke asked as Andy parked in the empty lot.

"A couple of my students are members here. They let us use the sanctuary a few times a year for these events. The acoustics are great, and it's less intimidating than a big recital hall."

Andy unlocked the door and led Brooke to the small room where the students would wait for their turns to play. She handed her a clipboard.

"Pete teaches piano lessons, and we join forces for these recitals since neither of us has a lot of students. There are sixteen numbers, and I've listed them here in the order they'll play."

She pointed to her neatly written schedule. "This gives you the student's name, age, and instrument. Also, this column lists what song they're playing and what music book it's from. They're supposed to have the pieces memorized, but there's always some last-minute panic, so you can let them see the music if they really seem scared. Here are the music books, and I've put tabs on the pages you might need, and I've cross-referenced the students' names so you can find the right song quickly."

Brooke looked at the clipboard and the pile of music books with little color-coded tabs sticking out of them. "My God," she said. "You are freakishly organized."

"I am not," Andy said indignantly. There was nothing freakish about being prepared. Her first recital, when she was seven, had been a disaster because she hadn't known what to expect. By her second one, she had her music organized, the right clothes picked out and clean. So now she made lists and schedules for herself and the parents involved, so her students could focus on their playing. "The kids are less nervous if everything runs smoothly."

Brooke just rolled her eyes as Andy continued. "Remember, these are little kids, so you need to make sure they're ready to go in the right order. No going to the bathroom if there's only one student in front of them."

"So how did you pick the order? Do they go by age, or level, or social security number?"

"Height, actually," Andy admitted. "It's less distracting if I'm not out there adjusting the music stand after every student. We alternate strings and piano to make it more interesting."

Andy gently pushed Brooke toward the first arrivals and slipped out of the room to check on Pete's progress in the sanctuary. She returned only moments later to find a red-headed boy tugging on Brooke's shirt.

"Lady, I really gotta see my music again," Andy heard him say as she walked over to rescue Brooke.

"No you don't, Bobby," Andy said. "You've been playing that piece without music for a month now. What's the first note?"

"An A?"

"Right. Once you have the first one down, the rest will come back to you. Now go get your viola ready for me to tune."

She turned to Brooke and smiled at her frazzled expression. "How's it going?"

"They're driving me crazy. I don't know how you do it."

Andy stepped closer and casually rubbed her hand across Brooke's back. "I usually have them one at a time, so it's easier. They get a little worked up on recital night."

"I'm beginning to think that one dinner isn't enough payment," Brooke informed her, leaning in to her touch. "I demand a raise."

"Anything you want," Andy said with a smile, brushing her body against Brooke's as she walked away. Brooke watched her go, feeling her body tingle where Andy had touched her. She shook her head and turned back to her clipboard, trying not to stare at Andy as she moved easily through the room, tuning instruments and cheerfully listening to her students. It was clear they adored her, and the kids clustered around her looking for encouragement and sympathy to help them through this ordeal.

Brooke spotted a small girl sitting in the corner. She didn't think she had checked this one in yet, so she walked over.

"Hi there. What's your name?"

"What's your name?" the girl echoed.

Brooke raised her eyebrows, but introduced herself first. "I'm Brooke."

"I'm Becky."

"Let's see, you're second to go. That's good, isn't it? Get it over quickly."

"I'm not playing tonight," the girl informed her.

"Well, you're on the schedule," Brooke said. "And you know how much Andy likes her schedules."

"I'm not playing," the girl insisted.

Brooke looked around desperately and caught Andy's eye. Andy handed a viola back to one of her students and came over to the pair.

"Good evening, Rebecca," she said formally. "Are you giving my friend Brooke any trouble?"

"She says she won't play tonight," Brooke informed her.

"Tattletale," Becky said. Brooke stuck her tongue out and made the little girl laugh.

Andy knelt down. "Why don't you want to perform tonight? You've been practicing a lot, and I know your dad wants to hear you play."

"If I play, something bad will happen," the girl whispered.

"Something bad?" Andy echoed. "What's the absolute worst possible thing that could go wrong tonight?"

Becky thought that one over for a few seconds. "I'll forget my song and pee my pants?"

Brooke covered her mouth in time to smother a laugh, but Andy managed to keep a straight face.

"Hmm, that is a bad thing. I'll tell you what, we have quite a few students playing tonight, so it's all right if you don't want to perform," Andy said. Becky sighed with relief, but it was short-lived. "When it's your turn, I'll tell the audience that you can't play because you won't remember your music and you'll pee on the church floor. They'll understand."

"You wouldn't really say that, would you?" Becky asked.

Andy shrugged. "I need to explain why you're not onstage. That's part of being a musician. Your audience comes to hear you play, and if you're not going to, then they deserve an explanation."

Becky struggled with that for a moment. Brooke didn't believe Andy would actually announce such a thing, but her face was dead serious, and if she were in Becky's position, Brooke wouldn't dare call Andy's bluff. Apparently Becky reached the same conclusion.

"I didn't say that would *probably* happen, just that it *might* happen."

"Oh," Andy said, her brow furrowed. "So what probably will happen?"

"My hands will shake and I might get some notes wrong."

"You know what?" Andy leaned over and whispered in a confidential tone. "Whenever I play for the symphony, that's exactly what happens to me. My hands get a little shaky, and I sometimes play the wrong note. But no one seems to care. They just like to hear pretty music."

"I guess I could try to play…"

"That's great, Becky. Now why don't you run to the bathroom before we start, just in case?"

The little girl trotted away, and Brooke finally let herself laugh. Andy stood up and smiled at her. Given Andy's thorough preparations for this recital, Brooke had expected to see her ordering the kids around like they were recruits at boot camp, but she hadn't seen any sign of Andy's need for control when she was interacting with her students.

"Remind me never to play poker with you," Brooke said.

"I never bluff. And please stop sticking your tongue out when I'm around. You're too tempting as it is."

With that she walked away and started gathering her students together. Brooke trailed behind and listened while Andy gave the kids a short pep talk and told them she would leave the door open so they could hear the other students as long as they were very quiet. She put her hand on Brooke's shoulder and reminded everyone that she would be in charge and they should do exactly what she said. The kids looked unconvinced, and Brooke did as well, but Andy seemed confident they would make it through the night with no major mishaps. Finally she left the room with the first grim-looking child. *One down, fifteen to go,* Brooke thought.

Brooke was able to watch most of the recital from her position in the doorway, but she spent more of her time watching Andy than the students. Most of the kids performed quite well, but after weeks of listening to Andy practice, the sounds of the beginning players were harsh even to Brooke's untrained ear. She found herself wincing a few times at a squeaky bow stroke or a glaring wrong note. Andy's expression never changed, though, and she smiled serenely through all of the performances.

She hung back after the recital as all of the parents and students wanted to have a chance to talk to Andy and hear her praise of the musical prodigies. A few of the smaller children, Becky included, even came over to Brooke to get a hug and have her meet their parents. She could feel Andy's eyes lingering on her, and she was relieved when they finally were able to gather up all of Andy's organizational supplies and head for the car.

It had started to rain while they were in the church, so they ran across the parking lot and jumped in the car, laughing and shaking the drops of water out of their hair. Andy sat back in her seat with a sigh, not moving to start the car right away.

"I'm glad to have that done," she admitted. "It's good for the kids but tiring to plan. You were such a big help tonight, and I really appreciate it."

"I kind of had fun," Brooke said. "But I'm definitely not applying for a job at a day care."

They sat in silence for a moment, the heavy rain and deserted parking lot giving them a sense of intimacy. Brooke felt a thrill of

HARMONY

nervousness, wanting Andy to kiss her yet dreading it at the same time. It seemed any time they started getting close they started to argue instead, so she cast around for a casual topic of conversation.

"I don't know how you do it," she finally said. "With all of your training and your ear for music, how can you hear some of those mistakes and not cringe?"

"When I first started teaching I would unintentionally make faces if my students messed up. All it did was make them nervous, and they'd concentrate on how I looked instead of their playing. I had to stop letting what I heard reflect on my face. It's mostly habit now, but sometimes I have to bite the inside of my lip. I know it's a bad recital if I make myself bleed."

"I'll have to try that next time," Brooke said with a laugh. "But it's more than how they sound. I guess I expected you to get upset if anything went wrong, but you didn't seem to mind if they forgot their music or went in the wrong order even though you had the evening planned perfectly."

"Perfection isn't what matters," Andy said with a shrug. "I plan the details so the kids trust me to know what's going on. If I yell at them for every mistake, they won't enjoy the music or learn anything. Those are the things that count."

Brooke silently wondered how many mistakes had been allowed in the Taylor household. "So, how about that sushi?" she asked out loud.

"A promise is a promise, I suppose," Andy said grudgingly, starting the car. She was smiling, though, and Brooke relaxed back in her seat as they drove. She had enjoyed watching Andy at work tonight. Seeing the evidence of her love of music and her desire to share it with her students had helped Brooke figure out some of the qualities she wanted in a job. Creativity, passion, the joy found when talent and work united. Brooke hoped she could find a career like that for herself someday.

Andy parked near the sushi restaurant and stopped the car. She reached over for Brooke's unresisting hand, lacing their fingers together.

"I really did like having you with me tonight," she said, her free hand brushing at a strand of hair that had come loose from Brooke's ponytail.

"Me too," Brooke agreed. She was all out of casual conversation, so she leaned toward Andy, and their lips met in a gentle kiss. Andy held back, not pushing the kiss too far, so it was Brooke who finally gave in and ran her tongue over Andy's lower lip.

"Ah, there's that irresistible tongue," Andy said against Brooke's mouth before taking it again in a much more passionate kiss. They broke apart after several minutes, both breathing heavily. The effect of having all of Andy's intensity focused on her was intoxicating to Brooke. She wanted to suggest they skip dinner and go straight home, but she knew it would only make Andy pull away again, like she did whenever they got physically close.

"We should get out of the car," Andy said, not sounding convinced at all.

Brooke sighed. "Your lips are dangerous, you know."

"Well, you're safe from me tonight at least," Andy informed her. "I'm not kissing you after you've eaten that disgusting raw tuna you like."

She dodged Brooke's playful slap and ducked out of the car into the rain.

CHAPTER THIRTEEN

"I have quartet practice tonight," Andy mentioned casually on Thursday morning. "Do you want to come with me? It only lasts a couple of hours."

"Sounds like fun," Brooke said as she handed Andy her latte. "There won't be any kids for me to chaperone this time, will there?"

"No kids, I promise," Andy said. She took a sip of coffee. "Mmm. Good, as usual. And since you've been doing so much cooking for me, how about I take you to dinner after? Italian?"

Brooke nodded with a smile and turned back to the counter. Instead of heading straight to her music room as she usually did, Andy waited while Brooke ground beans for her own coffee. She had tackled the easy topics, and she wasn't sure how to bring up the more sensitive one.

"I've asked my friend Jonas to come tonight," Andy said when the kitchen was quiet again. "I thought you might like to meet him."

"You're not setting me up with some guy, are you?" Brooke asked with a smile. "I thought you were asking me on a date."

"Of course not," Andy said quickly. "Jonas is David's—our cellist's—partner. And yes, I did ask you out. I just invited Jonas to come so the two of you could talk while we practice."

"Talk," Brooke repeated. She stopped fiddling with the espresso machine and leaned against the counter with her arms crossed. "About what?"

"About everything," Andy said, trying to ignore the chilly tone in Brooke's voice. "About the changes you've made. Calling off the wedding and moving in with me. And about where you want to go, how to move forward."

"And why would Jonas want to hear all of this?"

"He's a psychologist," Andy said. She had expected Brooke to react to the word, but she hadn't anticipated such a furious expression would come over her face, so she pushed on quickly. "He specializes in gay and lesbian issues, and helping people deal with coming out. He'll understand what you're going through."

"What I'm *going through* is fighting bossy and domineering people who want to take over my life!"

"I'm only trying to help you, not run your goddamned life," Andy said, her voice escalating in spite of her attempts to stay calm.

"You set up a therapy session behind my back, and you don't think that's crossing a line?"

"I just thought Jonas would be nicer than your other therapist. He won't try to tell you what to do or that your feelings are wrong."

"But it's okay for you to tell me what to do?" Brooke asked, pushing off the counter and glaring at Andy. "You're just like my parents."

"I am not like them at all," Andy said in a clipped tone. What the hell was she supposed to do? Watch Brooke struggle to make sense of her life without trying to help? Sit back and watch her withdraw until only occasional glimpses of a vibrant, fun woman showed through? "I hate to see you so sad."

Brooke shook her head with a humorless laugh. "You're so damned in control of your own life, you can't stop yourself from managing everybody else's."

Andy fought to steady her voice, desperate to end their argument. She certainly didn't feel in control of this situation, or any other that concerned Brooke. "I didn't hire Jonas as your shrink. He's just a friend, a nice man who's easy to talk to. No expectations. Hell, you can spend the whole time complaining about me, if you want."

"Then I'll need more than a couple of hours," Brooke said. Her arms were still crossed tightly over her chest, but her mouth turned up in a brief smile. "I don't like you thinking of me as a helpless child."

"God, Brooke, I don't," Andy assured her. "I think you're very brave. It took courage to call off your wedding, to defy your parents. I just don't understand why you insist on doing it all on your own. I didn't have anyone to talk to when I came out to my family, and I want it to be better for you," Andy said, pushing away the pain her old memories caused. "If you want, I'll call him and cancel."

"I guess I can try," Brooke said. "But if I'm not comfortable with him, I'm leaving."

"You can keep the car keys, just in case," Andy said with a relieved smile. She reached out and gently brushed Brooke's arm before she left the room. Brooke didn't pull away from her touch, so Andy hoped they had at least made a temporary peace.

❖

Andy finished packing up her instrument and music, and came into the hall just as Brooke emerged from the bathroom. She stopped in surprise at the sight of Brooke in the blue blouse and earrings she had bought on her first day at Andy's apartment.

"You look amazing," she said, her admiring eyes roaming over Brooke. "That color is perfect for you."

Andy reached out to run her finger over one of Brooke's dangling earrings, careful not to touch her skin.

"Thank you," Brooke said quietly. Andy turned away to find her car keys, and her composure. The sight of Brooke, apparently dressed up for their date, unwound the tension Andy had been feeling since their argument and sent her headlong into desire. She couldn't seem to be around Brooke and feel anything neutral. Every emotion had to be extreme and disconcerting to her ordered world. She slipped into her coat, shoving her hands in its deep pockets to hide their slight tremble.

The drive to Richard's college, where the group met for practice, took only a few minutes. Both women were silent, each locked in her own thoughts. Andy still struggled to shake off the remaining effects of their fight, and she guessed Brooke was still angry, and maybe a little anxious, about meeting Jonas. They parked next to the music conservatory, a beautiful brick building with white columns, and Andy led the way inside.

"Wow," Brooke said as they walked through the main entrance. The small foyer led to a three-story-high open space with an arched ceiling. The classrooms and offices ranged around the perimeter of the performance area.

"The sound is great here," Andy said, pausing with Brooke as she turned slowly in the center of the space. "We sometimes play in here if the building is empty."

Andy and Brooke headed to a practice room on the second floor. Muted sounds from piano and voice students wafted through several of the closed doors. Andy's group was already in the room when they entered.

"Hey everyone, this is Brooke Stanton," Andy said, her hand on the small of Brooke's back as she led her forward. She felt a small surge of pride as she introduced Brooke, but she reminded herself it was unfounded. She was simply introducing a friend, not a girlfriend, to her colleagues. "This is Richard Harris, first violin, Tina Nelson, second violin, and David Sidhran, cello."

Richard shook her hand formally while David gave her an infectious smile and wave from his seat across the room.

"October Fifth, nice to finally meet you," Tina said as she shook Brooke's hand. Brooke gave Andy a questioning look.

"We refer to brides by their wedding date," she said, giving Tina a glare that was gleefully waved off. "It's less confusing that way."

"Do you need to change my name since the wedding didn't happen?" Brooke asked, earning an approving smile from Tina.

"No," she said. "We'll just add a question mark to it and call you 'October Fifth?' until you decide what comes next."

Brooke laughed, but Andy quietly wondered if she had any hope of being included in what came next for Brooke.

"Jonas is in my office," Richard said, looking up from the music he was marking with a pencil.

"Thanks," Andy said, shaking off her gloomy thoughts. "C'mon, Brooke. Let's go see him."

They walked in silence to Richard's third floor office. Andy tapped on the half-open door, and a tall, thin man with longish hair and rimless glasses looked up with a smile.

"Andy, good to see you again," Jonas said, rising from his chair and giving her a kiss on the cheek. "And you must be Brooke."

Brooke shook his hand warily. "I am. And you should know I'm here under protest. Andy ambushed me"

"I said I'd cancel if you wanted," Andy snapped.

Jonas stepped between the two women. "Andy, go practice. Now," he added when she didn't move. She reluctantly left the room, and Brooke turned her glowering face to Jonas.

"You have every right to feel angry," he said in an infuriatingly calm voice that made Brooke want to slap him. He grinned as if reading her thoughts. "You're free to go, of course, or we can sit here and talk for a few minutes. You're not a patient and I'm not your doctor, but if you'd like an objective friend, then I'm here for you."

"Why?" Brooke asked suspiciously.

"Because I like Andy," he answered simply. "And she likes you."

Brooke struggled between the desire to just walk out into the night and leave all of them behind, and the insistent need to freely talk out her worries. Two years with her therapist had convinced her that this crap didn't work, but something about the open look in Jonas's eyes made her want to give him a chance. She slammed down in the chair, still angry at Andy.

"Fine," she said in a clipped voice. "We can talk."

Jonas laughed and shut the door. "She's going to pay for this, isn't she?"

"I'll find some way to make her suffer."

"I'm sure you will," Jonas said as he sat on the opposite side of Richard's desk. "You know, Andy is the one who holds this quartet together," he said with a shrug as if saying something insignificant. "She keeps the emotional brides happy and the temperamental musicians in line. It's important for her to keep things tidy and peaceful, and that's why she is the group's liaison with the public."

He laughed. "At first they tried to alternate which of them met with the brides. Richard is a nice guy and a brilliant musician, but he was so stiff and condescending that he made his bride cry. David doesn't take anything seriously, and I love him for that, but he had his poor bride so confused with his jokes that she ended up agreeing to have the quartet play 'Pop Goes the Weasel' as she walked down the aisle. Tina saw it as a personal challenge to sleep with hers before the wedding." Jonas paused and gave her a wink. "Andy only did that once, that I know of."

Brooke blushed, and he continued. "It's not just her job to keep everyone happy and calm, it's who she is. And if she needs to manipulate people, in a kind way of course, to keep the peace, then she'll do that. And now you've come into her life, bringing chaos and change and sadness, and she doesn't know how to handle it. I've never seen her lose her temper like that."

"Are you saying I'm bad for her?" Brooke asked with a sinking heart. She might be furious with Andy for tricking her, but the thought that she might be making Andy miserable was devastating.

"Of course not," Jonas laughed. "I think you're exactly what she needs. A little mess in her life."

Brooke returned his smile. "I certainly am that."

About an hour later, Jonas suggested they rejoin the quartet in the practice room. "They're playing one of David's compositions tonight, and I haven't heard it yet," he said, his love for the cellist apparent in his voice.

They slid quietly into the room, not wanting to interrupt the group as they played through a series of Beatles songs that had been requested for their next wedding. Brooke sat in her chair and listened to the rendition of "And She Loves Me," stubbornly refusing to meet Andy's eyes when she glanced over. Her anger had worn away as she had talked to Jonas about Liz and Jake and Andy, but it didn't seem fair to let her off the hook just yet.

What really rankled Brooke was that Andy had been exactly right about her need to talk to someone understanding and sympathetic. There was none of the pressure or judgment that had been so much a part of her other therapy experiences. She had been most surprised by Jonas's ability to bring laughter into their conversation. She had been taught to see therapy as something stuffy and humorless, but she was able to laugh and relax, finally talking to Jonas like an old friend.

Looking back, Brooke knew her former therapist had been trying to cure her, clearly judging her feelings for Liz as wrong, or at least misguided. Jonas hadn't challenged either her feelings or her decisions but instead gave her concrete advice about what to expect as a result of her choices, and how to talk to others about them. She had spent so many years hiding different parts of who she was from different people—her sexuality from her parents and Jake, and now her growing attraction from Andy. Jonas had no personal stake in her life choices, so she felt able to speak freely with him. He was able to describe the coming out experiences of other people, including his own as a teenager, and he managed to make her feel less alone in a way those closest to her couldn't right now.

Jonas nudged her when the quartet started to play David's composition. She had expected a silly, light song from the irreverent cellist, so the somber melody caught her off guard. Even to her untrained ear, it was obvious David had composed the music with his quartet in mind, and each instrument had its turn to play melody. She listened in awe as Andy's viola soared through an intricate passage, the other instruments backing her up with the harmony. She was startled out of her fury enough to spontaneously applaud with Jonas when the last notes from Richard's violin died out.

After David made a few notations on his pages of sheet music based on their feedback, the group chatted about the composition and about their upcoming events as they slowly put their instruments away. Brooke watched Andy interact with the rest of the group. She talked easily with them about music, but fell silent when the discussion turned more personal.

"Does everyone have big plans for Thanksgiving?" Tina asked.

"Nancy and I usually visit my family in Boston, but she won't be able to fly this year," Richard said. He turned to Brooke. "My wife is seven months pregnant," he explained.

Brooke still didn't know what she'd be doing for the holiday since Andy refused to take her home. Suddenly Brooke's mind clicked and she smiled inwardly at her idea. *Ambush me, will you?* she thought. *Then it's payback time.*

"Andy and I were planning a Thanksgiving dinner for just the two of us at her apartment," she said sweetly. "We'd love to have all of you join us."

While three members of the quartet enthusiastically jumped at the offer, and began discussing what each could bring, Andy stared across the room at Brooke, her expression shocked. Brooke finally met her gaze, still keeping her expression carefully neutral.

"When exactly did you start planning this?" Jonas whispered in her ear.

"About two seconds ago," she said, and then raised her voice over his laughter. "It'll be vegetarian, of course, for Andy."

❖

They drove in silence to the Italian restaurant Andy had chosen. It wasn't until they had placed their orders and had a carafe of wine on the table that Andy trusted herself to speak civilly to Brooke.

"You know I have to go home for Thanksgiving," she said, downing half a glass of wine in one gulp. "Now all of these people are expecting to come to my place. What am I supposed to tell them?"

"I wonder if my friend Jan really needs to go to California to see her family," Brooke said. "I think she and Tina would like each other."

"I'll have to cancel, so don't invite anyone else."

"Andy, listen to me," Brooke leaned across the table and waved a breadstick at her. "I'll admit I asked everyone just to make you mad, but it's a great idea. They're your friends, and they are excited to spend time with you. Wouldn't it be more fun to be yourself there than to go to your parents' and pretend to like men, turkey, and Amy?"

"More fun, maybe," Andy reluctantly agreed. "But if I don't go home, my dad will be furious. And my mom…"

"Your mom has chosen to stay with him all these years. Even if you go home and keep the peace that one day, I'm sure he finds other reasons to lose his temper during the year. You can't control his anger."

Andy struggled with that for several minutes, fidgeting with her wine glass until their food arrived. She had to admit that Brooke was right. She usually avoided a lot of social interaction with her quartet members, but they had seemed genuinely enthusiastic about the idea of getting together for the holiday. And she would get to spend the day with Brooke instead of with her ulcer-inducing family. Yes, she would take just this one holiday for herself, since it might be her only one with Brooke in her life. As a small sign of apology, she offered Brooke a forkful of her pasta with baby artichokes in a caper and lemon sauce.

"Mmm. I could totally make that," Brooke sighed. "I'd give you a taste of my risotto, but it has pancetta in it."

"Truce?" Andy asked hopefully.

Brooke speared another bite of artichoke and nodded. "I think we're even."

"So, are you going to tell me what you and Jonas talked about?"

"No, and I'm not going to tell you that you were right to bring us together," Brooke informed her, swiping a piece of bread through Andy's piccata sauce.

"Should I just move my plate to your side of the table?" Andy asked with a laugh, pouring more wine into their glasses.

"Well, that would make it easier for me to eat," Brooke admitted without a trace of guilt. She spooned up some more risotto and slipped her hand over Andy's where it lay on the table. "Thank you," she said, more seriously. "Jonas and I talked about coming out and how hard it can be to go through it alone, without someone to talk to, to trust. Thank you for being there for me." Brooke pulled her hand back. "But you need to remember that if I lean on you for support, it doesn't give you the right to pick me up and carry me where you want me to go."

"I'd do anything to help you," Andy said quietly, a little frightened by the truth of her statement. She wanted to reach for Brooke's hand again, but common sense stopped her. Brooke was in transition, and while she might need Andy now, she wouldn't depend on her forever. Brooke might leave, and when she did, Andy wondered who would be around to rescue her.

CHAPTER FOURTEEN

A ndy happily tucked her viola in its case after Saturday
night's concert. Her section had played the difficult piece
flawlessly, helping to showcase the solo violin, a fourteen-year-old
Polish prodigy, and she allowed herself to feel just a little proud of
her part in their performance. She knew a strong first chair could
really set the tone for the other players, and she was glad the hours
she had spent perfecting her timing for this piece had been noticed.
Several of her violists had complimented her on leading them so
strongly through the concerto, and the conductor had even nodded
in her direction as the curtain closed.

Andy pulled on her coat and followed the other musicians
out of Benaroya Hall and into the chilly Seattle night. The energy
around them was electric, and they were all caught in the high of
a well-received performance and the brush with a spectacular new
talent. She sighed as she separated from the group and went to her
car, feeling the adrenaline of performance slowly seeping away. She
would have loved to spend this evening with Brooke, sharing her
thoughts about the concert, maybe going back to Mickey's for a
drink. Maybe a dance…

Andy shook herself mentally. *Give it up,* she thought. Brooke
was out to dinner with her parents and Jake tonight, somewhere in
Everett so they were less likely to run into their snobby friends.
Andy would have been tempted to skip tonight's concert just to go
with them and support Brooke, but she hadn't been asked. Besides,

she was fairly certain Brooke had chosen this night because of the symphony's schedule. Andy knew Brooke didn't want to have her there as a crutch, but she worried Brooke couldn't hold up under the pressure of the three people who had such an influence on her. She wouldn't be surprised if they simply bundled Brooke back home just like they did from Gonzaga, sending someone for her things tomorrow.

Andy was unlocking her car door when a hand slid around her waist. She gave a quiet shriek and jumped to the side, barely rescuing her viola case before it banged her car.

"You scared the hell out of me!" she shouted as she turned to find Lyssa laughing at her startled expression. "You don't sneak up on people in dark parking lots."

"Sorry," Lyssa said, not looking sorry at all. "I did call your name, but you were so deep in thought you didn't hear me."

Andy jerked open her trunk and gently set her viola case inside, securing it with straps so it wouldn't jostle during her drive. She busied herself with the instrument while she caught her breath. She hadn't talked to Lyssa since the day she had been picked to play Clarke's sonata. She felt rattled by the scare, Lyssa's close presence, and the memory of her insulting words. When she felt slightly more collected, she closed the trunk and turned toward Lyssa.

"Pretty horrific concert, wasn't it?" Lyssa asked, leaning against the car door and blocking Andy's escape. "That girl should be playing on a street corner, not in Benaroya, don't you think?"

Andy sighed. That was her cue to agree with Lyssa's jealous, untrue critique, then to cajole her by saying that of course no one could play better than Lyssa could.

"What do you want, Lyssa?" she asked instead, too tired for the game.

Lyssa's neat eyebrows arched in surprise, and then she nodded with an understanding smile. "I see. You're still angry about what I said when you got your Clarke solo." She stepped forward, her hand sliding under Andy's coat and up to cup the back of her neck. "I'm sorry, baby. You know I didn't mean it like it sounded. I was having a bad day, and I guess I took it out on you."

Andy pulled Lyssa's hand out of her hair, hoping her own wasn't shaking too badly, and stepped around her to unlock the car door. "It doesn't matter," she said, irritated because her voice revealed just how much it *had* mattered. She turned to face Lyssa again. "I have to get home."

Lyssa sighed. "Stop being angry, it's making me weary. Some of the other players are going to Mickey's for a drink. Come with us. It'll give us a chance to talk and sort this out."

Andy wavered between the need to get away from this woman and her reluctance to return to an empty apartment. She glanced at her watch and figured Brooke wouldn't be home for at least another hour. If she came home at all. Sharing the success of the night's concert with her friends would help the time pass.

"I guess a drink wouldn't hurt," she said, making Lyssa's face light up. "Do you need a ride?"

"No, I have my car. I'll see you there," she said, laying her hand briefly on Andy's cheek.

Andy drove the short distance to Mickey's. She would have preferred to walk and clear her head, but the symphony's lot would close soon. She found a parking place next to Lyssa's sports car, and they went into Mickey's together, Lyssa linking her arm companionably in Andy's. Andy felt a strange sense of peace with Lyssa's familiarity. These past weeks with Brooke were like a dream—wanting her, waiting every day for her to choose to stay or leave. Lyssa, the symphony, her music, these were the things that belonged in Andy's world, and they were all she'd have left if Brooke went away.

Andy went up to the bar to order her beer and Lyssa's cosmo, torturing herself by leaning across the stool that Brooke had sat on just a few weeks before. She was startled by a wave of loneliness and wondered if Brooke missed her too, or if she felt a tug toward the safety of her old life like Andy did. Andy scolded herself. *Just give it up.* It was too painful to keep worrying about Brooke tonight, especially since she had no control over Brooke's choices.

She turned from the bar and spotted Lyssa at a table for two near the dance floor. She carried the drinks over and sat down.

"I don't see anyone else from the symphony," she said, eyes narrowing as Lyssa attempted to look innocent.

"Huh," Lyssa said, looking around as if surprised. "I guess they took the long way."

"We're fewer than ten blocks from the hall," Andy said, smiling in spite of her irritation at being tricked.

Lyssa shrugged and managed to appear faintly apologetic. "I lied, okay? You haven't spoken to me or looked my way for weeks now." She reached across the table and grasped Andy's hand. "I miss you."

Andy didn't pull her hand away, enjoying the contact in spite of her effort not to. She wished it were Brooke here, touching her, as confident in what she wanted as Lyssa always was.

They held hands and talked, only letting go when Andy returned to the bar for fresh drinks. By the third beer, her mind was feeling a little fuzzy, and she found herself relaxing, talking and laughing with Lyssa as if there hadn't been any friction between them. She had been obsessed with tonight's concert for the past few days, studying the counting and dynamics at night and practicing for hours. Her nervousness at this first real test of her ability to lead her section had kept her from eating much today, so the beer went quickly to her head.

She accepted Lyssa's offer of a dance, pushing the image of Brooke in her black tank top out of her mind and replacing it with one of Brooke sitting to eat with her family. That made it easier to pull Lyssa into her arms, with all the familiarity of an old lover, and hold her close as they swayed to the slow music.

"God, I've missed *this*," Lyssa moaned, pressing close and sliding her arms around Andy's neck. Andy tightened her hold on Lyssa's lower back, making her arch so her breasts pressed against Andy's.

Andy's eyes were closed, but she knew without looking that most of the other women in the bar would be watching her with envy. Lyssa, with her long, pale hair and confident bearing, was model-beautiful. A small, hateful part of Andy thrilled at the knowledge that she had the ability to shake this gorgeous woman's controlled demeanor, making her beg and scream as she neared climax. Andy's resistance broke, and when Lyssa raised her head for a kiss, she was only too willing to acquiesce.

The slow song ended, and a throng of people entered the floor for the next fast dance. Andy grabbed Lyssa's wrist and pulled her roughly into the darkened hall leading to the bathrooms. She pressed her against the wall, continuing the kiss they had started on the dance floor, her tongue delving into Lyssa's open mouth as her hand found Lyssa's breast. They broke apart for a brief moment, both breathing heavily, barely aware of the people moving past them. Lyssa took control this time, taking Andy's hand and tugging her into the bathroom and locking them in the farthest stall.

"I need you," she whispered in Andy's ear, pulling her satin skirt out of the way as Andy's hand reached between her legs. Her nylons ended at the top of her thighs, and Andy's fingers easily pushed past Lyssa's lacy underwear to find her wet and ready.

Her tongue thrust into Lyssa's mouth again, and her mind raced forward as she orchestrated the best way to make Lyssa climax. After so many times together, she knew all of the right ways to please her. She would take her quickly and strongly, forcing her to abandon her façade and scream with the pleasure of release. And then Lyssa would be satisfied, energized. Her ego restored after tonight's virtuoso performance by the young violinist. And Andy would be left where? Wanting, needing some sort of release, flooded with guilt over betraying Brooke. She broke away suddenly, tugging her hand out of Lyssa's underwear as if she had been stung.

"Why are you stopping?" Lyssa gasped, her breath ragged. "Please, I need—"

"It's all about what *you* need, isn't it? Well, I can't do this anymore," Andy said in a shaky voice. She ripped off some toilet paper and wiped her hand, flushing away the used paper. She desperately wanted Brooke here, Brooke who had spent their only night together accepting what Andy offered, but then willingly giving pleasure in return.

She shouldered past Lyssa, who clutched at her arm. "Please, Andy," she begged. "Don't leave. I can make you feel good too."

"Why start now?" Andy asked roughly, jerking the door open. "You've had four years to try."

She walked quickly through the bar, grabbing her coat and leaving before Lyssa could catch up. Guilt stalked her as she got in her car and drove off quickly. Not guilt about Lyssa, who probably already had a line of women knocking at the bathroom door after Andy's abrupt departure. She would find what she needed tonight without any problem. Instead Andy agonized over how she would tell Brooke about this, what it would mean to their undefined relationship. Even if Brooke didn't return tonight, Andy knew she shouldn't have been in another's arms without knowing of Brooke's decision. And she knew without a doubt, whatever happened between her and Brooke, she was through with Lyssa's games and needs.

❖

Andy entered her apartment and froze at the sight of Brooke sprawled across the sofa bed, surrounded by magazines and dressed in one of Andy's old T-shirts. Her face looked tired, but she smiled when Andy entered the room.

"How did the concert go?" she asked immediately.

"Fine," Andy answered briefly, although she could barely remember the music that had seemed so important a few hours ago. Now all she knew was guilt.

"I knew it would. I'm getting some ideas for Thanksgiving dinner," she said, gesturing at the glossy cooking magazines. "I think I'll try to make a pumpkin pie from scratch."

"Do you mean from-a-can scratch, or are you planning to disembowel a real pumpkin?" Andy asked, shifting her viola to her other hand. Brooke must have been practicing on her these past weeks, slowly carving away until Andy's carefully ordered insides had turned to mush.

"A real one," Brooke said, and then raised her hand to stop Andy's comments. "And don't you dare say it sounds messy. The kitchen will be a disaster after all this cooking so you'll have to just—"

"Deal with it?" Andy suggested.

"Exactly," Brooke said with a smile. She patted the bed next to her. "Come over here and help me decide what else to make."

"I'll be right there," Andy said, taking her viola to the music room. She washed her hands and quickly changed into sweats, her relief at seeing Brooke again warring with her need to admit that she had kissed Lyssa. She went back into the bathroom and splashed cold water on her face, taking a few moments to pull herself together. Her mind had turned to Brooke so often tonight, and thoughts of her were muddled with Andy's memories of kisses, soft breasts, the smell of sex. She had mistakenly started something with Lyssa, and she wanted nothing more than to finish it with Brooke.

Brooke shoved a few magazines aside to make room for Andy. "How was your dinner?" Andy asked tentatively as she sat on the bed. Brooke shrugged.

"Jake and I went alone. I couldn't face him and my parents at the same time," she said, a note of sadness in her voice. "It wasn't easy, but once we got started, we talked about everything. I told him I think I'm gay. He's hurt, but I think he's a little relieved as well. He was worried there was something wrong with him since it never seemed right between us. He promised to keep it to himself for now, so I can tell my parents when I'm ready."

Andy brushed her thumb along Brooke's cheekbone, wanting to wipe away the stress she saw on her face. "I was worried you would go home with them," she confessed, dropping her hand back into her lap.

"I guess I'm not finished seeing Switzerland yet," Brooke said shyly, staring at one of her magazines before she raised her eyes to Andy's. "What is it? What's wrong?" Brooke asked with concern. "You're sure the concert went okay?"

Andy nodded her head. "It really went well, and the soloist was amazing. The audience loved it."

"I'm glad. I know how hard you worked for this one. Did something else happen tonight?"

"Do you remember the first time we met? In the coffee shop?" Andy asked, evading the question momentarily. Brooke nodded without interrupting. "You asked if I had a boyfriend and I said…"

"That you had a 'sort of' girlfriend. Yes, I remember. I was… Oh." Brooke's face fell. "Did you sort of hook up with her tonight?"

"Something like that," Andy admitted. She took a deep breath and told a silent Brooke about her past affair with Lyssa, and the whole night's story.

Brooke listened to it all, wincing at the details Andy wanted to leave out but knew she couldn't. "I don't have any right to—" she started when Andy had finished her confession.

"Yes, you do." Andy said quietly.

"No, I can't expect you to just wait until I decide—"

"Yes," Andy insisted, placing a finger under Brooke's chin and turning her head so their eyes met. She wanted Brooke to claim her, to claim their relationship. She was afraid any possessive words would make Brooke panic, but she had to be clear about her feelings. "Yes, you can. I want you to expect that. I'm so very sorry for what I did. I have no idea where we're going, but I'll hate myself if I ruined our chances. Please say you can forgive me?"

"Of course I forgive you. We've never defined what's happening between us, and I'm not ready to make a commitment yet when there are still so many loose ends. You didn't break any rules," Brooke said. Unshed tears reddened her eyes, however, and her quiet voice almost killed Andy. "It's not like we're together."

"God, please don't say that," Andy whispered, closing her eyes. They sat in silence while Brooke ripped tiny pieces off a magazine cover and Andy simply wallowed in her guilt.

"I'm no different, am I?" Brooke finally asked.

"What do you mean?"

"You've done nothing but give to me since we met. I'm just like Lyssa. I've taken it all and done nothing in return."

"You're not serious?" Andy asked, shocked. "The two of you are nothing alike. And I'm the one who kissed her, don't you dare turn the blame on yourself."

"I'm not. But look at what you've done for me. You've given me a home, friendship, faith in myself. What have I given you? Clutter?"

"Companionship."

Brooke rolled her eyes. "A bathroom you can barely squeeze yourself into anymore."

"The best lattes I've ever had."

"An ulcer."

"I don't have an ulcer," Andy said. "And even if I do, you're not the sole cause of it."

Brooke slapped at her, a little of her playfulness returning. "Can I make an unreasonable demand?"

"Anything," Andy said with such conviction that Brooke's breath caught in her throat.

"Jake gave me until Christmas to decide. I'm not going back to him, and he knows that now. But will you give me the same offer? Until Christmas to decide if I can be with you? We can date each other, but no other women until then?"

Andy gently took her hand and gave it a squeeze. It might kill her to give this woman her heart and still have her leave in a month or two, but she only felt relief that they still had a chance together. "You have my word."

CHAPTER FIFTEEN

Andy came home from work a week later just as Brooke was coming out of the shower wearing only a towel. Although her exhausting holiday schedule helped keep her mind off Brooke to some extent, Andy wasn't too tired to want to rip that towel off and drag Brooke to her bedroom.

"Andy, wait," Brooke said. Andy had been trying to escape to her music room until Brooke could get dressed, but she stopped with a sigh.

"What's up?" she asked, keeping her gaze focused on Brooke's eyes and not letting it drop any lower.

"I noticed you don't have anything scheduled on your calendar for Sunday night."

"Nope," Andy said with a grin. "No concerts, no weddings, nothing."

"I need to get out of this apartment. Can I kidnap you?"

"Of course. Where are we going?"

"It's a surprise. Be ready to leave at five, and dress warm."

Andy didn't normally like surprises, preferring to be prepared before she went anywhere, but this was the first time Brooke had offered to plan one of their dates. Andy was curious to find out what she would pick for them to do. No amount of cajoling or threatening could make Brooke give up her secret, so Andy took her cue from Brooke's clothes and came out of her room a little before five wearing jeans and a polo shirt with a bulky sweater over it.

Brooke drove, taking I-5 out of Seattle and heading south to the small town of Kent. While they drove, Andy listened to Brooke's account of her latest interviews. The number of people looking for work meant employers could be choosy, and Brooke's meager experience didn't make her a prime candidate. Her search was discouraging, but Brooke made all of their meals and insisted she buy the food as well. Andy would gladly have accepted just her cooking skills, but Brooke felt better if she was contributing more. Plus, it eased the pressure of the job hunt, giving her a chance to find work she would enjoy.

When they pulled into a parking stall at ShoWare Center, Andy looked around and then back at Brooke, her eyes reflecting her confusion.

"We're going to see a hockey game?" she asked.

Brooke laughed at her expression. "Yes. Come on, it'll be fun."

She pulled a reluctant Andy along with her as they joined the crowd entering the arena and stopped at a concession stand. Brooke ordered a couple of beers apiece and a huge bag of popcorn.

"Do you want a jersey, or one of those foam fingers?" Brooke asked.

"Thanks, but I'm good," Andy said, surprised to see Brooke so at home among the rowdy fans.

"Let me know if you change your mind," Brooke said as she led the way to their seats in the first row.

"Wow, we're really close," Andy said, peering through the Plexiglas at the smooth ice.

"I know. Great seats, aren't they?" Brooke agreed enthusiastically.

"If you say so."

Brooke handed her a beer and the bag of popcorn. "Don't tell me you've never been to a hockey game before."

"Never," Andy said. She usually found team sports too chaotic to watch or play. "I did see that movie about us beating the Russians in the Olympics, though."

"Then you'll love this."

"Yeah, it's practically the same thing. Seattle versus Portland is just like watching the United States playing against Russia during the Cold War."

Brooke punched her in the arm. "This is a serious rivalry, you know."

"Sorry. I wasn't aware the honor of my city was at stake. If I had been apprised of the gravity of this situation, I would have taken you up on the offer of a foam finger."

"I should buy one and make you wear it to pay for that sarcasm. Hockey is no joking matter to me. I used to play on a team, so I know how important these games are."

"You. Played. Hockey." Andy shook her head in disbelief. All the time they had known each other, Brooke had been in turmoil. Andy realized she was getting a peek at the real Brooke, the one she'd be after her life settled again. And she liked what she saw— she liked the fire, the passion, the hint of aggression.

"I played until junior high. Then my mom decided it wasn't ladylike enough, so I had to take ballet instead. I didn't understand why she thought it was just a sport for boys when I was in an all-girl league, but she found it rather horrifying to watch me play."

"I can picture you tearing around out there, whacking at other kids with your stick. And your poor mom, watching her budding lesbian roughhousing on the ice."

Brooke laughed. "At the time I didn't realize I was a budding anything. But I did have a huge crush on my coach. I always volunteered to help with the equipment so I could be near her. Maybe I should have recognized the signs back then."

"But they were so subtle, who could have guessed?" Andy asked with a laugh. "What did your dad think of your hockey playing?"

"He loved it. He'd go to my games and scream at the refs and the coach so much that it was surprising he didn't get kicked out. We used to come watch the Thunderbirds together sometimes. I saw the Spokane Chiefs play a couple of games when I was at Gonzaga, but I haven't been to a game since then."

"I'm glad you brought me," Andy said honestly. Not neces-sarily because of the game, but because she liked to see Brooke having fun. She worried sometimes that Brooke had been more focused on what she needed to do—find a job, pay her share, make choices—than on what she wanted. But now, Brooke was smiling and leaning on the armrest between them so her shoulder and arm were pressed against Andy's. She could put up with watching men skate around with sticks for a couple of hours as long as Brooke stayed close.

Andy ended up enjoying the evening more than she had anticipated, however. Brooke's excitement was infectious, and although Andy didn't share her tendency to yell at the players and referees, she found herself rooting for the Thunderbirds along with the crowd. Brooke explained the rules, which didn't seem too complicated, so it was easy enough for her to follow the game.

She almost dropped her beer the first time two players slammed against the Plexiglas right in front of them, but after a few times she got used to it.

"Cool, huh?" Brooke said with a grin when a member of the opposing team was smashed into the wall like a bug.

"God, who are you?" Andy asked in amazement.

"So I like sports. The subject just hasn't come up before."

"Well, I have to admit this new side of you is weirdly sexy."

Brooke pressed closer. "You think so?" she asked before turning her attention back to the game and booing with the crowd when the referee sent one of their players to the penalty box.

Andy laughed, distracted by Brooke until the Plexiglas rattled again, startling her enough to make her drop some popcorn. "I think that number twelve guy likes you. That's the third time he's hit the wall in front of us."

"I thought he was flirting with you," Brooke countered. "I swear I saw him grin at you."

"Was that a grin or a grimace of pain?"

Two hours seemed like a long time to score a measly three points, but at least the home team won. She and Brooke filed out with the boisterous fans and got into Brooke's car. Before Brooke could start the engine, Andy leaned over and kissed her on the mouth. This definitely qualified as a date, and while Brooke might have asked her out this time, Andy couldn't wait for her to make the first move.

"Thank you for tonight. I had fun."

"Good. I'll get us tickets for another game," Brooke said, kissing Andy again before she could protest. This kiss lasted longer than the first, and Brooke reluctantly withdrew her fingers from Andy's hair and sat back. She'd originally asked Andy to the game because she didn't want to go alone, even though she'd guessed it wasn't something Andy would normally choose to do. She had hoped Andy would be a good sport and not sulk about her choice of activity, but she hadn't expected Andy to show so much interest—not necessarily in hockey but in Brooke, in her passions and her childhood.

Andy smiled at her. "If this is how every game is going to end for us, I'll buy season tickets."

CHAPTER SIXTEEN

Andy came home from teaching to find Brooke at her dining room table, typing rapidly on her laptop. "Any calls?" she asked. Brooke didn't turn around, so Andy walked over and tapped her on the shoulder.

Brooke jumped and pulled out the earbuds she had been wearing. "You scared me," she said accusingly.

"Sorry, I just wanted to know if anyone called," Andy said.

"Richard. He's booked two more weddings," Brooke answered, handing Andy a piece of paper with the information scrawled on it.

"Thanks," Andy said, her glance taking in the tables and bulleted lists on Brooke's screen and the psychology reference books next to her. "What are you writing?"

"It's my new job," Brooke answered, a hint of pride in her voice. "I'm doing transcription work for some of the doctors in Jonas's office. He brought it over today."

"You don't mind doing it?" Andy asked. She knew Brooke hated not working, even though her job search and cooking added up to a full-time job.

Brooke shrugged. "It's pretty simple and kind of fun. They record their notes, and I listen and type them out. I can work at home, on my own time, so I can keep looking for what I want as a career. After all those years of therapy I'm familiar with most of the terminology, so at least I'm getting some good out of that experience."

"Well, I'm glad for you," Andy said, her hand just brushing Brooke's shoulder. She didn't know how she could be so hurt by this woman and yet be so relieved to see her happy.

"You don't mind that I borrowed your laptop?"

"Of course not," Andy said absently as she tried to read Richard's message. "They're lucky you're not doing that longhand, or they'd never decipher it. Is this woman named Dollie?"

Brooke glanced at the note. "Debbie."

"Okay. And this one wants us to play a song called 'Furbise'?"

"'Fur Elise,' by Beethoven," Brooke said indignantly, snatching the note from Andy and scrawling two words across the page. "Can you read that?"

Andy laughed and ruffled Brooke's hair. "That one is pretty clear. Same to you, by the way."

"You also got a call from a woman in the symphony's education department," Brooke said as Andy headed into her music room to call her brides.

"What'd she say?" Andy asked, hesitating in the doorway.

"She said you can invite students or friends to the rehearsal for this concert. They're having a short lecture about Bach and the Brandenburg Concertos."

"Well, thanks. I'll let my students know."

"I want to go."

"I already got you a ticket to go to the concert, Brooke. It'll be the same music and the same lecture beforehand if you want to hear it."

Brooke crossed her arms and frowned. "I'd like to go. It'll be interesting to see you at work."

Andy frowned back. "Whatever," she said crossly and shut herself in the music room. She wouldn't admit to Brooke that she was afraid of making a fool of herself onstage. They were performing the sixth Brandenburg Concerto as a small ensemble piece, and Andy would have significant solo parts with only a handful of other instruments playing alongside her. At the concert, she might be able to get away with a small mistake here or there and the audience probably wouldn't notice, but at the dress rehearsal the conductor would be ready to call her out for any tiny error. The thought of Brooke sitting in the audience while she butchered her first solo part as principal viola made her want to throw up. She could try to talk her out of going, but she knew a losing battle when she saw one. Besides, Brooke had probably already signed herself up.

❖

"Aren't you ready yet?" Andy called, banging on the bathroom door. Brooke swung the door open calmly and walked out, a subtle cloud of perfume floating after her.

"You said we don't need to be there for another hour," Brooke said as she slipped into her shoes and then gestured at her outfit. "Is this appropriate?"

"You look beautiful," Andy said simply, too wound up to prevaricate. "I love you in that color."

Brooke mumbled a thank you, turning away from Andy's gaze to put on a jacket over her navy dress shirt and gray slacks.

Andy led the way out of the apartment, stopping in frustration when she noticed that Brooke wasn't following her.

"Now what? Don't tell me you need to check your hair again."

Brooke looked surprised by Andy's sharp tone. "I may not have your years of musical experience, but isn't it common practice to bring your instrument when you're going to play in a concert?"

"Sorry," Andy muttered as she stomped into the music room for her viola. "Thank you."

"No problem," Brooke replied smoothly. "But I think I should drive us there."

Andy didn't argue with that one, and she sat in the passenger seat and fidgeted until Brooke reached over and grabbed her hand.

"You'll be great," she said, giving Andy's hand a squeeze. "You've practiced the hell out of that piece. And I've heard it so many times I'll be able to hum it for you if you lose your place."

Andy smiled briefly and cradled Brooke's hand in her lap, their fingers twining together. "Thanks. I guess I'm glad you forced me to bring you tonight."

KARIS WALSH

"Smart ass," Brooke said.

"Nice ass," Andy mumbled, turning to look out her side window with a more relaxed grin.

Brooke parked in Benaroya's garage, and Andy walked her to the lecture room. Brooke gave her a quick kiss on the cheek before she headed backstage.

"You'll be fine," she whispered, but Andy didn't look convinced.

Brooke settled in with the mix of adults and younger students and listened to the lecture that touched the baroque era, Bach's life, and the music they were going to hear. The lecturer talked about the varied groupings of instruments that had been used in the past to perform each concerto, and he explained how the conductor had chosen the ensembles for this performance. It was interesting enough to keep her from worrying excessively about Andy, and she was a bit surprised that the time to file into the main hall came so quickly. Once seated there, however, she felt as tense as if she were about to perform herself. She didn't know how Andy could stand waiting until the end of the program for her concerto.

Unlike other concerts Brooke had attended, this was a working rehearsal, and the conductor occasionally stopped the performance to make some changes or had the orchestra play passages over again to correct timing or dynamics. Each concerto had a different number and grouping of instruments, and several featured one or more soloists. She watched, mesmerized, as Andy played through three of the concertos, from the first with its strings, woodwinds, and horns, to the third with only a small string section and harpsichord. During the brief intermission, the conductor reworked a section of the second concerto, drilling the four soloists on their entrances. The violinist was a stunning blonde who played with a relaxed confidence. Brooke didn't need to look in her program to know that this must be Lyssa Carlyle, Andy's "sort of" girlfriend. She tried to ignore the stab of jealousy she felt when Andy joined in the applause after Lyssa played.

She had to suffer through more of Lyssa's flawless playing since the fourth and fifth concertos featured the violin as well, first with two recorders then with a flute and harpsichord. Finally it was

Andy's turn, and Brooke felt a rush of excitement as she rose and joined a small group of musicians at the front of the stage. There were only two violas, a cello, and a bass, plus two period instruments that Brooke recognized as violas de gamba, thanks to the lecture. There was an air of professional aloofness about Andy that seemed foreign to Brooke, but once she started to play, she turned back into the Andy she knew. Her expression and posture softened as she launched into the ornate first measures of the piece, and Brooke relaxed with her as the viola's deep voice sang out the notes she had heard coming from the music room so many times. All too soon she was clapping loudly with the rest of the audience.

Once the final concerto was finished, Andy returned to her seat, and the conductor gave the players a few final notes before they started to pack their instruments away. Brooke joined some other audience members who were climbing onto the stage to visit with various players. She was heading toward Andy, who waved her over while she was chatting with another violist, when a woman called her name.

"Cindy, hi," Brooke greeted the tall woman. If she had managed to drag her eyes off Andy and Lyssa this evening, she would have noticed her friend on stage. "I forgot you played with the symphony."

"Flute," the woman said, holding up a small black case as proof. "Did you enjoy the concert?"

"Very much," Brooke said.

"We missed you at book club this month."

"Oh, you know how it is," Brooke said evasively. Cindy was the only person from her guest list she'd seen since cancelling the wedding. She wondered if there was some rule of etiquette about which of them should bring up the awkward subject first.

"I'm sorry about you and Jake," Cindy said. She paused, but Brooke didn't offer more than a polite smile. "So, who do you know in the orchestra?"

"Oh, um, Andy Taylor is a friend of mine. She invited me to come tonight," Brooke answered. *Sort of,* she amended in her head. She glanced over at Andy who was now talking to the beautiful blond soloist.

"She did a great job tonight."

"She did, didn't she?" Brooke said proudly. "I should get going, but it was nice to see you again."

"You too. I hope you'll make our next meeting."

Brooke promised to try and hurried over to Andy and the blonde. She felt a twinge of jealousy at the sight of the two musicians. They made a striking pair, one so fair and the other dark and serious, and both so talented.

"…messing up the rhythm in such a simple piece. Maybe you should try practicing with your metronome so you don't do that in front of a real audience." Brooke only caught the end of Lyssa's comment, and it took her a moment to realize that she was criticizing Andy's performance in that snotty tone. She felt a rush of protective anger and for once acted without worrying what the people around her might think. She marched up to Andy and slid her hand up to the nape of her neck.

"You played so well tonight, babe," she said, pulling Andy's lips to hers in a fierce kiss. Even in her confusion over Brooke's actions, Andy couldn't help but respond to her touch and kiss her back. She pulled away, her brow furrowed as she tried to figure out why Brooke was suddenly acting like a lover.

"Brooke Stanton, Lyssa Carlyle," she said briefly, noticing Lyssa's angry red cheeks.

"Oh, hi," Brooke said casually as she shook Lyssa's hand. "Didn't you play a solo, too? It sounded pretty good. I know this cold weather can make it hard to keep your instrument in tune."

Andy bit her lip to keep from laughing at Lyssa's furious expression. She was saved by the conductor who asked to see all the soloists for a few minutes after the rehearsal.

"Ms. Carlyle, Ms. Taylor, are you planning to join us?" he called impatiently,

"Be right back," Andy said to Brooke, squeezing her arm lightly.

"Good," Brooke said, tracing a finger down the buttons of Andy's white shirt. "And when we get home I'll show you just how proud I am of you."

Andy turned away, fighting to keep a straight face as she and a fuming Lyssa walked over to the conductor. Brooke sat in Andy's chair next to her viola case wearing a smug smile.

Andy returned shortly and grabbed her case and Brooke's hand. "Let's get out of here," she said, tugging Brooke to her feet. "I don't want the two of you getting in a fight in the middle of the stage."

"I hope you didn't mind that kiss," Brooke said. "But I heard her insulting you, and it just made me so mad I had to do something."

"Well, the gesture was a bit overdone, but appreciated, *babe*," Andy said, dropping Brooke's hand once they had left the stage. "She was right, though. I rushed the tempo of my sixteenth notes."

"I really did think you were wonderful," Brooke said, bumping against Andy's side and getting a smile in return. "Is she always so bitchy about other people's playing?"

"Well, yes. And she's still mad at me for walking out on our, um, conversation a few weeks ago," Andy explained. "It made her feel better to criticize me, but it doesn't matter." She shrugged, realizing that for once it was true. Lyssa's words hadn't hurt her feelings or her self-confidence. "I know what I did wrong, and I'll play better at the concert."

"I'm sorry for what I said about tonight, about when we get back home," Brooke stammered. "I didn't mean we really should…"

"I know," Andy said, staring straight ahead as she walked to the car. "You have a flair for the dramatic, Brooke. It's not a secret around here that I'm a lesbian, so you just came out on stage, in front of the entire orchestra."

"I know," Brooke echoed Andy's words. "I'm sure Cindy can't wait to tell the book club. But it was worth it to watch Lyssa turn so red."

Andy finally let herself laugh at that. "I especially liked the part about the weather. Did you notice that she was retuning her violin when we left the stage?"

Andy stowed her viola in the trunk, feeling strangely lighthearted after the evening's stresses. Brooke had come running to her rescue. And that support had helped Andy break free of Lyssa's ability to erode her confidence.

"Thanks again for intercepting my phone call and inviting yourself to the rehearsal," she said, leaning back in the passenger seat as Brooke drove them home.

"Ooh, such a gracious way to say thank you," Brooke said.

"You have a better way in mind?" Andy asked.

"You can buy me dinner," she answered haughtily, pulling the car into a parking spot near one of their favorite restaurants on Broadway. "I feel like Mexican food."

CHAPTER SEVENTEEN

Andy spent nearly as much time in the bathroom getting ready for the concert as Brooke usually did. She finally came out to find Brooke curled on the couch with a book.

"Do I look all right?" Andy asked nervously, fidgeting with the outfit that she only wore during the holiday season.

"Very nice," Brooke said as her eyes raked over Andy's black outfit, from her slim velvet pants to her silky blouse. She stood and casually adjusted the collar of Andy's top, her eyes as bright and unrevealing as crystals.

"You, too," Andy said, her mouth suddenly dry at the sight of Brooke in her simple black dress with its expensive-looking cut. She couldn't seem to stop from reaching out and moving her hand along Brooke's hip, feeling the black lace overlay slide on the satin lining.

Brooke frowned slightly and took Andy's hand from her hip. "Come in here for a minute and let me fix you," she said, tugging on Andy's hand to get her to follow into the bathroom, ignoring her protestation that she didn't need to be fixed. She propped her against the counter and took a bottle of hair gel off the counter.

"There. Much better," Brooke said with a short nod after she rubbed the gel on her hands and raked them through the sides of Andy's hair. She turned her to face the mirror.

"Wow," Andy said, staring at her reflection in surprise. With the sides slicked back and her bangs a little spiky from the gel, she had a more put-together look than before. The style swept the hair from her face so the angles of her cheekbones and her arched brows were accentuated. Her eyes met Brooke's in the mirror. "I like it."

"I told you there's more to hair care than a bottle of shampoo and a comb," Brooke said, giving Andy a quick kiss on the neck.

Andy turned away to hide her desire at Brooke's simple kiss. "C'mon. We'll be late."

They were silent as Brooke drove them to the hall, holding hands like they had on the way to the dress rehearsal. When they parted company in the hall's garage, Brooke put her hands on the sides of Andy's face and looked her in the eyes.

"You'll be great tonight," she promised, giving her a brief kiss. "I'll lead the standing ovation."

Andy smiled grimly and lugged her viola backstage, pushing thoughts of Brooke and that kiss out of her mind as she mentally reviewed each section of the night's program. She realized in a moment of panic that she had completely forgotten the first measures of her own concerto, and as soon as she entered the room where the other players were warming up she started searching for the sheet music.

"I do hope you got that timing problem corrected," Lyssa said, standing over Andy as she pawed through her case. Andy's eyes traveled up the length of her, unable to keep from registering how the harsh black outfit suited Lyssa, making her fair skin look like porcelain. She watched a similarly reluctant look of admiration cross Lyssa's features when she noticed Andy's hair.

"Yes," Andy said shortly, mentally adding that she had the timing down, but had apparently forgotten most of the notes. "And I presume that you've got your violin in tune?"

"Why don't you worry about your own playing. Too bad my solos aren't after yours so if you mess up, the audience could still leave on a good note."

She walked away, and Andy was left to wonder where all of her confidence from the night before had gone. She finally found her music and flipped it open, hoping a quick refresher would jog her memory. There was a brightly colored sticky note on the first page of the sixth concerto.

"Stop worrying, you haven't forgotten the notes," Brooke had written in her barely legible handwriting. Andy smiled and closed the score, suddenly not feeling so alone. Damn, but it felt good to have someone know her so well and to be there at exactly the right time.

The musicians were given their fifteen-minute notice, so Andy hurriedly tuned her viola and played a brief warm-up. Once onstage, she stuck Brooke's note on her music stand underneath the score. Although she couldn't hope to see past the bright stage lights and find Brooke in the audience, just knowing she was out there believing in her gave Andy the confidence to get through the night. As a seasoned orchestra player, the Brandenburgs were very familiar to her, so she easily played through the first five concertos. She had never had a chance to play the sixth for a paying audience, but she managed to get to her place in front of the orchestra without falling over, her knees shaking only slightly. Once she started playing, the notes seemed to fall from her viola without much effort on her part. Her tempo remained steady, and the six instruments bounced the music back and forth like an intricate game of catch. She couldn't help smiling broadly as they finished, and she saw her expression mirrored on the other players' faces.

As well as it had gone, Andy was relieved when the concert finally came to a close. Her shoulders and jaw ached from the extra tension she had held all evening as she concentrated on getting every aspect of her playing right. It was all she could do to carry her viola case to the car.

Brooke was waiting for her with a huge smile that helped to melt some of Andy's tension. Brooke gave her a hug and pried the viola case from her hand.

"Let me," she said with a small frown. "You look exhausted."

"I'm all right," Andy assured her, watching to make sure her viola was carefully stowed away. "Just the normal let down after a concert. You helped, though. How did you know I would panic about forgetting the notes?"

Brooke laughed. "Lucky guess. You doubt yourself more than anyone I know, and you have less reason to."

They were getting in the car when another viola player walked by. "Great job tonight, Andy," she called. "Will we see you at Mickey's?"

Andy shook her head. "Thank you, but I think we'll pass tonight. See you next week."

Brooke started the car. "Is it because of me? I heard you say no after the dress rehearsal as well."

"It's not you," Andy assured her. "I'm just too tired tonight. There are a few of us who meet at the bar sometimes after rehearsals or concerts, but I don't go every time. We can if you really want to."

Brooke shook her head. "I'd rather get back to the apartment."

They drove in silence, and Andy was worn out enough to allow Brooke to carry her viola up the stairs. She disappeared to take a long, hot shower while Brooke made up the sofa bed. Andy came out in her sweats to say good night, but Brooke gestured at the table next to the couch.

"I brought you a beer," she said. "Come sit with me for a little while."

Andy thought the beer would help her relax, but sitting in bed with Brooke definitely would not. She felt too wound up to go straight to sleep after the stress of the day, however, so she pushed aside her common sense and sat on the edge of the bed. They made small talk about the concert and some of the other players until Andy started to lose some of her tension. She brought them two more beers from the kitchen and leaned more comfortably against the back of the sofa.

"I could give you a back rub," Brooke suggested. Andy gave her a look of alarm and she laughed. "I'm not planning to molest you," she said. "But you keep rubbing your neck like it's sore. Come here."

Andy reluctantly moved between Brooke's legs, her back held stiffly to avoid any contact with her.

Brooke leaned toward Andy's ear. "Relax," she demanded as her fingers started to knead Andy's tense muscles.

She worked across Andy's shoulders, feeling her slowly give in to the gentle pressure and lean in to the massage. Andy groaned quietly when Brooke found a knot of tension, and Brooke felt her own body respond to the sound. She moved her hands to Andy's upper arms, then to the front of her shoulders, pressing Andy back against her.

"Brooke, what are you doing?" Andy asked, still not resisting Brooke's touch.

"Just giving you a massage," she answered, rubbing her hands under Andy's collarbones and barely touching the swell of her breasts. "Please, let me make you feel good."

"You do, and that's the problem," Andy said. As worn out as she was, Andy found the strength to stop Brooke's hands before they reached her breasts. Dating her was fun, and their occasional kisses were wonderful, but Andy couldn't go any further until Brooke knew what she wanted. She twisted around to give Brooke a kiss and then reluctantly pulled out of her arms.

"Thank you for being there tonight, Brooke," she said, trying to ignore the desire she saw mirrored in Brooke's eyes. She went into her bedroom before she could change her mind.

Chapter Eighteen

The Monday before Thanksgiving, Andy emerged from her music room earlier than usual. Brooke was at the dining room table, making yet another list of ingredients for her dinner.

"Hey," Andy said, resisting the urge to cross the room and give Brooke a good morning kiss. Since the concert, her desire to touch Brooke had been growing stronger, fueled by the knowledge that Brooke wanted her too. She had to keep her distance until Brooke decided whether she wanted Andy for keeps, or just for a night. She busied herself at the sink instead, washing her coffee mug. "I don't have lessons today since it's a holiday week. Do you want to go to Pike Place and get some food for Thursday?"

"I'd love to," Brooke said, waving the piece of paper she had been writing on. "I have the menu finalized, so we can get our produce there at the market, then stop at Whole Foods on the way home for the rest."

"Sounds good," Andy answered, glad to see the excitement in Brooke's eyes. Her mood seemed to be lifting as Thanksgiving approached, and Andy wanted to encourage that as much as she could. Even if it meant turning her small kitchen into a disaster area.

The fall day was clear but chilly, so Andy pulled a fisherman's knit sweater over her T-shirt then grabbed her car keys. Normally she wouldn't drive downtown for a shopping trip, wanting to avoid the hassle of city parking, but she figured Brooke would have too many bags of groceries for them to comfortably carry on the bus.

She was winding a scarf around her neck when Brooke came out of the bathroom.

"What's wrong?" she asked, as Andy avoided her eyes.

"Nothing," Andy said. "You look very nice."

Brooke looked down at her navy turtleneck sweater and jeans. "Really? I thought this outfit seemed a little ratty," she said, tugging at the hem of her sweater. Andy made a strangled sort of sound as Brooke's movement made her turtleneck pull even more snugly across her breasts. She slapped lightly at Brooke's hand.

"Stop doing that," she said. "You're driving me crazy." Andy held Brooke's windbreaker for her to put on, but she didn't move toward it.

"Do I need to change?" she asked, confused. "You're looking at me like I'm wearing my underwear on the outside."

Andy sighed. "I'm looking at you like that sweater shows every curve of your body and makes your eyes look like incredibly blue diamonds," she said, flapping the windbreaker slightly to make Brooke move. Brooke turned and slipped her arms into the jacket. "And your ass looks amazing in those tight jeans," Andy added, giving her a playful swat. She was rewarded with one of Brooke's laughs and a light kiss on the cheek. Those little intimate gestures, when Brooke acted like they were a couple, turned Andy on more than any overtly sexual move ever had.

Andy drove toward Puget Sound, luckily finding a parking place on one of the side streets near Pike Place Market. There were people everywhere, and they jostled their way among the masses, Andy only occasionally placing her hand on Brooke's back to keep them from getting separated. She was careful to drop the contact immediately once they were in a more open area. Although Andy didn't like the crowds, they were worth enduring just to feel Brooke's mood change. Everything about her became more animated, from her gestures to her walking speed, and her interest flickered rapidly from one subject to the next. This Brooke was such a different woman from the one Andy first met, sitting alone in the coffee shop, closed off from the world around her. They wandered aimlessly, checking out the produce stands stocked by local farmers and peering at the bakery display cases. The breeze off the Sound was getting colder, so Andy steered them into the covered section of the market.

"I used to come here with my grandfather when I was little," Brooke said, a contented smile on her face as she stopped to take a taste of some locally harvested honey, picking out a subtle hint of blackberries in the sweet aftertaste. "I remember how exotic it seemed, with people speaking different languages, and the smells of spices and fish and salt water. I used to pretend we had sailed to a foreign country. Ooh, look!"

She darted across the aisle with Andy in tow and accepted a piece of organic pear from a vendor who was cutting up samples. "Wow, try this."

She fed Andy a bite of her pear, using a finger to wipe away some juice that caught in the corner of her mouth, lingering there a moment before she withdrew. It was such an innocent touch, perfectly safe in public. Brooke's thoughts were anything but.

"It's very good," Andy said.

Her voice gave nothing away, but when Brooke saw Andy touch her tongue to the spot where Brooke's finger had rested, and then smile, Brooke had the suspicion that Andy felt the same desire she did.

"Do we need pears for Thanksgiving?" Andy asked.

"No, but we should get some while we're here." Brooke shrugged, paying the farmer for a bag of fruit. *So I can feed them to you when we get home,* Brooke added silently. She handed it to Andy. "Now, isn't there a cooking store around here? I need some pans."

"As your regular dishwasher, I beg to differ," Andy muttered, but she pointed across the street. "There's a place right up here, and it's next to a nice wine shop."

Now that they were acclimated, they started shopping in earnest. She and Andy argued good-naturedly over the pattern of serving dishes, spent over half an hour debating which local wines to pick, and reached simultaneously for the same bouquet of flowers for the table. They were shopping together like a couple, Brooke decided, and the thought worried her. She enjoyed their comfortable rapport and could hold her own in any decision they made, but she worried she was getting too relaxed with Andy. Would she be able to separate herself from Andy's stronger presence when it came to bigger decisions than what color napkins to buy? Brooke's concern over their easy domesticity made her self-conscious about the closeness she felt with Andy. Every time they touched, she would lean into the contact and then pull away quickly. Occasionally their hands would brush, and Brooke would feel Andy's fingers start to tighten on hers before she suddenly discovered something she needed to touch or pick up. The crowds and the constant push and pull of their connection were starting to exhaust her, and seemed to be wearing on Andy as well.

"If you're going to treat me like a pack mule, you should at least feed me something," Andy growled as Brooke slipped another bag of produce over her arm. Brooke glanced at her face, startled by her tone, but when Andy spoke again the traces of irritation were absent from her voice. "There's a place on the next street that has great Mediterranean food," she suggested.

"That sounds good," Brooke said. "I'm starving."

"How can you be hungry after you've sampled half the market?" Andy asked with a laugh. "You're like a two-year-old. Everything you see goes in your mouth."

"Hmm. I thought you liked that about me," Brooke said with a grin, resettling the small sugar pumpkin she carried under her left arm and hooking her right hand under Andy's elbow. She pulled her hand away again and moved the pumpkin back to her right side.

"It happens to be one of your best traits, if I remember correctly," Andy said. "And you know, you can touch me."

Brooke bumped Andy with her shoulder, just hard enough to knock her off-balance. "How's that?"

Andy took a few awkward steps with her heavy packages but managed to stay upright. "That wasn't what I meant by touching," she said, taking a swipe at Brooke with the bag of wine and narrowly missing a man who was trying to pass them. He stepped off the sidewalk and glared as he walked past. "See?" she said to a giggling

Brooke. "He probably wouldn't have noticed if we had just been holding hands."

Brooke, still laughing, moved her pumpkin again and slid her arm through Andy's as they walked the short distance to the restaurant. "I'm only doing this to keep you from knocking over any pedestrians," she said.

Andy dropped into a seat at one of the street-side tables surrounded by their bags, while Brooke went into the restaurant, barely the size of Andy's kitchen, and ordered their food. After sharing a plate of falafel with tahini sauce, sitting close enough to Andy so their thighs brushed under the table, Brooke's spirits were improving rapidly. She relaxed enough to get sidetracked by the flavors as she scooped up the last bits of saffron rice with a piece of pita bread, and she decided they needed to return to a spice shop they had passed so she could try to recreate the meal.

They were almost out of the market when Brooke veered off again, following the smell of cinnamon to a kiosk selling doughnuts.

"Granddad and I used to get these," she said once Andy had caught up. They watched the tiny doughnuts drop into the fryer, and Brooke bought a bag for them to share.

Brooke popped a doughnut, still warm from the oil, into Andy's mouth since her arms were too laden with bags for her to eat on her own. Andy was watching her as if mesmerized while Brooke licked cinnamon-sugar off her fingers, until her gaze suddenly shifted to a point over Brooke's shoulder. Brooke turned to see what had caught Andy's attention, but at first all she saw was a crowded seafood stand. "It's funny that almost every TV show about Seattle shows those guys throwing fish around. I don't get why…" Her voice faded as she saw Jake standing with a couple of people from the office. They were laughing and talking as if trying to entertain Jake. She watched silently for a moment. "That's Marianne and Steve from the law firm," she said finally.

"Do you want to go talk to them?" Andy asked reluctantly, breaking Brooke out of her trance.

"No." She shook her head and turned back to Andy. "Jake and I have talked enough. I don't think we're ready for a casual meeting in public."

Brooke knew it would upset Jake to run into her when he was with his friends, to be pitied as the jilted lover. She balled up the bag with the last two doughnuts in it and tossed it in a garbage can on the way to the car. She had saved him from an awkward meeting, but she felt her own day clouded with reminders of the past.

❖

They finished shopping and drove home in near silence. Brooke knew it hurt Andy when she withdrew like she had this past hour, but her mind was too full of guilt and indecision to make the effort to return to the lighthearted mood they had shared all day. They both seemed to be dragging as they hauled the groceries up to Andy's apartment. Andy set their bags on the counter and went to check the answering machine.

"Call me." The angry tone of the simple answering machine message startled both women.

"My dad," Andy said grimly, heading toward her room to make the call. "Do you mind putting the groceries away while I call him back?"

Brooke shook her head and started to unpack the mountain of produce that had looked so good at the market. Now she wasn't sure if she had the energy to do all the cutting and chopping and cooking that were required to assemble the food into a meal fit for company. She put the pears that had seemed so sweet and wonderful this morning into a bowl on the dining room table and wished she could step back in time and relive this day that had been full of laughter and teasing. This time she wouldn't turn around and see Jake looking so dejected, and have to face the realization that she was the cause of his heartache. She was sorry about his pain, but she knew she had made the right decision. Seeing him, she realized how little she missed her old life, and it frightened her how close she had come to subjecting them both to an unhappy marriage. She had been so blind to her own needs, and she couldn't let that happen ever again.

Brooke winced as she heard Andy's voice rise in the other room. With the door closed, she couldn't hear the conversation, but Andy's tone told her it wasn't a pleasant one. Brooke's heart reached out to her, and she realized Andy offered a kind of relationship so different from what she had with Jake. Andy recognized and appreciated all of those wacky little traits that made her Brooke. And just being with her made even something as simple as buying groceries playful and fun. And most of all, Brooke had a nearly irresistible urge to touch her and be close to her.

Once all the food was haphazardly thrown into the fridge, Brooke sat at the dining room table and listened to the sound of Andy's voice as she dealt with her father's anger. He must have been told, probably by Amy, that his oldest daughter wasn't coming home for the holiday this year. Apparently he wasn't accepting the fact calmly. After over half an hour, there was only silence from Andy's room. Brooke waited several minutes, then tapped lightly on the bedroom door and opened it to find Andy lying on her bed.

"Hey, sorry I didn't help with the groceries," Andy said quietly, rubbing her eyes with the heels of her hands.

"It's all right," Brooke said as she sat on the edge of the bed. She reached out and gently brushed Andy's hair back from her face. "Was he very angry with you?"

"You could hear?"

Brooke shrugged. "Not much. It's my fault this happened. I was trying to get back at you when I invited everyone for Thanksgiving, and I didn't realize—"

Andy grabbed Brooke's hand that was still playing with her hair. "You did a nice thing. Everyone's looking forward to coming. It's just that, dealing with him when he's so mad, I feel like a little kid again. I'd rather be here with you on Thanksgiving, but I hate disappointing my family."

"It seems the more we try to be happy, the more we hurt other people," Brooke said sadly. Andy couldn't deny it. She knew that without her there as a buffer, Amy and her dad would be at each other all night. She didn't know how she could enjoy Thanksgiving if she knew her family was miserable, but she couldn't hurt Brooke after she had worked so hard to plan a great holiday for everyone.

"I can make us something for dinner," Brooke offered after a short, depressing silence.

Andy shook her head. "I'm not hungry. But could you lie here with me for a while?"

Brooke nodded, and they stripped down to T-shirts before sliding under the covers. Brooke turned on her side and pulled Andy against her, wrapping an arm tightly across her waist. Andy felt the warmth of Brooke drawing the tension out of her body. Just this morning, being this close would have triggered an arousal that would have kept her awake all night, but now Andy only wanted to relax into the comfort of Brooke's arms. A couple of months ago, she'd had some semblance of control over her life. Her relationships with Lyssa and her parents weren't ideal, but they were familiar and predictable. Her work with the symphony was uninspiring but enjoyable. Now she was being pushed out of her comfort zone with her new symphony role of leader and soloist. Her professional life was encroaching on her personal life. In fact, it was coming to Thanksgiving dinner. And this woman had come into her life bringing complications and an untidiness that threatened the thin veneer of harmony she had been fighting to maintain. Andy drifted to sleep in Brooke's arms, wondering why it felt so right to be with her, in spite of all the chaos she brought.

Chapter Nineteen

B rooke cooked for two solid days, in a frenzy of activity. She desperately wanted to give Andy a taste of Thanksgiving that was full of good food and friendship instead of deception and conflict. Once she started the massive project, however, she felt her own mood lift as the smells and tastes of her creations filled her with a sense of accomplishment. The pumpkin pie was indeed the kitchen disaster Andy had expected, and Brooke couldn't clearly explain how she got pumpkin seeds stuck on the ceiling, but judging by the pie's aroma it promised to be worth her effort.

Andy spent most of the days in her music room or at the symphony hall, preparing for the usual rush of Christmas concerts. She told Brooke she was putting in extra hours of playing so she could have Thursday free without guilt, although she emerged now and then to taste one of Brooke's experiments or help with chopping vegetables. Their meals consisted of small samples of Thanksgiving dishes and a large bowl of couscous that Brooke decided was good enough for them to eat, but not for company.

It wasn't until Thursday morning that Andy went into a frenzy of her own and started cleaning the apartment. Brooke glowered at her as she made their lattes, not pleased about waking up at seven to the sound of the vacuum. Andy ignored her usual good morning cheer and carried armloads of Brooke's clothes into her room and dumped them on the closet floor.

"I was going to sit in bed and read with my coffee," Brooke complained when she saw that Andy had folded up the sofa bed.

"Sit on my bed," Andy said without compassion. "Then get your shower out of the way before I box up most of the stuff in the bathroom."

Brooke opened her mouth to protest, but Andy spoke before she had a chance. "You can have everything back tomorrow, but for today it's going in a box under the sink."

By noon, they had each done as much as possible to prepare for their guests. "This is the last of the couscous," Brooke said as she dropped onto the sofa next to Andy and handed her a plate. The dining room table was already set up as a buffet for dinner.

"Now I know what to be thankful for," Andy muttered as she toyed with her food before resignedly putting a bite in her mouth.

❖

Andy came out of the bathroom a few minutes before their guests were due to arrive, buttoning the dark green shirt she wore with khaki pants, her hair still damp and slicked back from her shower. Brooke stood by the stove dropping chickpea fritters into a pan of hot oil. She was barefoot and wearing a skirt because she told Andy she wanted to show off her tattoo.

Andy came up from behind and slipped her arms lightly around Brooke's waist, only tightening her hold when Brooke leaned back into her embrace.

"The apartment smells like a spice market," Andy murmured, nuzzling Brooke's neck. "And so does your hair." The exotic scents combined with the traditional Thanksgiving scene seemed so appropriate for Brooke, Andy decided. Always unique, and always unexpected.

Brooke fished the browned fritters out of the pan and turned in Andy's arms, slipping her own around Andy's neck.

"You smell like shampoo and toothpaste," she said, brushing noses with Andy. Andy's hand slid up Brooke's back and into her hair. "Why don't we call everyone and cancel?" she asked as she lowered her mouth to capture Brooke's.

Brooke felt Andy's body tense when the knock on the door interrupted their tentative kiss. "It's going to be okay tonight. They're your friends."

"I know," Andy muttered through clenched teeth. She reluctantly let go of Brooke and went to answer the door. There was a knot in her stomach, familiar to her after years of traditionally miserable holidays. She grimly anticipated an evening of stilted conversation and constant effort on her part to keep everyone somewhat peaceful and entertained. She wanted nothing more than to keep the door shut and hide inside, alone with Brooke who had been so soft in her arms.

She opened the door for Tina and her latest girlfriend. She took their coats, trying to place the tall and elegant black woman whom Tina introduced as Alison. She took them in to meet Brooke before heading toward her bedroom with their coats.

"That's it," she said with a snap of her fingers as she turned back to the kitchen. "You were November Ninth's maid of honor."

Alison looked at Tina, who frowned at Andy and then explained the quartet's way of naming brides.

"Don't worry about it," Brooke told Alison with a grin as she nudged Andy playfully. "I was October Fifth."

Their laughter helped ease some of Andy's tension, and she stepped into the role of host, pouring drinks for her guests and answering the door when Jonas and David knocked. She and Alison were arguing with the guys about what music to put on Andy's stereo when Richard and Nancy arrived.

"Hey, I thought this was supposed to be a vegetarian dinner," David said to Richard who was helping Nancy with her coat. She was petite except for her enormous pregnant belly. "Are you trying to smuggle in a turkey?"

Even as he joked with them, David gently helped Nancy into a comfortable chair. She sighed as she sat down and patted her stomach.

"It feels like a twenty-four pounder, at least," she told him. "We'll be able to feed the whole apartment building."

Andy made introductions before disappearing into the kitchen to prepare more drinks. When she returned, she stood quietly in the doorway for a couple of moments, observing the scene in her living room. Tina and David sat near Nancy, laughing and shrieking as she regaled them with gruesome stories about the childbirth video she had watched at her Lamaze class. Alison and Richard had taken charge of the stereo and were sifting through Andy's music selection. Brooke and Jonas sat on the couch, talking like old friends.

Andy stepped in and handed a cranberry juice to Nancy and one with vodka to Richard.

"Thank you," he told her before responding to something he heard his wife say. "I did not faint when we saw that film," he said loudly over David's gleeful laughter.

"The instructor had to get you a cold cloth and help you with your breathing," she said with a shake of her head. "I'm supposed to be the one lying back on the pillows and being fussed over."

Brooke slipped over to Andy who was standing a little apart and watching the good-natured banter between husband and wife.

"You're smiling," Brooke said, stepping close to her. Andy wrapped her arm around Brooke's shoulders and pulled her close. Brooke gave her a quick kiss on the mouth. "Now, go talk to your friends while I check on dinner."

Andy joined Jonas on the couch, and soon the two of them were discussing favorite hiking routes in the Cascades. The small group of people filled Andy's tiny apartment, but instead of feeling claustrophobic, as she had been expecting, the atmosphere was cozy and warm. People moved around, forming various new groupings as the conversation flowed, and she found herself letting go of the need to oversee every discussion in order to keep the evening free of dissension. She heard Richard and David arguing about Bach across the room, but soon they were laughing together without needing her as a referee.

She headed into the kitchen and found Brooke and Tina leaning against the counter talking and drinking wine.

"Hi," Brooke said, lighting up at the sight of Andy. Tina looked from one to the other and rolled her eyes.

"I'll leave you two alone," she said. Neither Brooke nor Andy tried to make her stay, so she took the wine bottle with her and went to the living room to refill glasses.

"I came for more hors d'oeuvres," Andy said, putting the empty plates on the counter. "Everything is delicious." She swiped a skewer with pieces of glazed veggie sausage and apple on it while Brooke refilled the plates.

"Mmm, I love these things," she said, taking another one. "What a great flavor combination."

"There's sage in there, too," Brooke said, slapping Andy's hand away as she reached for a third appetizer. "Save some for the guests."

"But I'm hungry," Andy complained. Brooke caught her eye at that, and Andy could see her breathing quicken. She took hold of Brooke's wrists and gently pinned her against the fridge. "I need to eat *something*," she complained.

Brooke bit her lip as Andy nibbled along her collarbone and then moved up toward her mouth, sliding her body up along Brooke's. She hesitated, their lips almost touching, and looked questioningly into those icy blue eyes. Brooke made the first move, closing the gap between them and kissing Andy. Andy responded with all the pent-up need she had been feeling.

"Time for dessert already?" David's jocular voice broke through their deepening kiss. "I just came in to find out what was keeping the appetizers, but maybe I should knock next time," he continued, picking up two of the refilled plates. "You have a sticky note in your hair," he whispered to Brooke before he walked out laughing.

Andy untangled the note and put it back on the fridge. She smoothed Brooke's hair with her fingers, then trailed them across her lips and down her neck, feeling Brooke's speeding pulse. "I should get back out there. Unless you need me to help with dinner?"

Brooke laughed. "I think if you stay in here and help me any more, our guests will go hungry." She turned Andy and gave her a push toward the living room. "Dinner should be ready in fifteen minutes."

❖

Andy eventually relaxed enough to realize she didn't have to do anything at this party. After years of holidays spent worrying over what she said or did, she discovered the joy of being with people who didn't have expectations of her that she could never quite guess, never quite live up to. Her last remaining concern, that her friends wouldn't enjoy the nontraditional food, lingered, because she knew her vegetarian diet had dictated Brooke's menu. She felt responsible for the food, even though Brooke had made all of it, but her worries vanished as she watched plate after plate consumed by their guests.

After eating, they all sprawled in the living room, too full to do more than compliment Brooke on the meal and listen to the Chopin etudes that Richard had chosen for them. Brooke was in one of the armchairs, her bare legs tucked under her skirt. Andy sat on the floor in front of her, leaning back as Brooke's fingers played through her hair. The room was in chaos, with paper plates, leftover food, and empty glasses on every surface. The difference between this and her usual Thanksgiving dinner with her family was striking. Instead of a sit-down dinner with cloth napkins, fine china, and stilted conversation, they had opted for a buffet. Everyone ate and laughed together, going back for seconds and thirds when they wanted, sitting wherever they could find a spot. On the surface it seemed less organized and controlled, but the depth of friendship and comfort in Andy's apartment filled her with a sense of peace she hadn't known for a long time. She draped her arm across Brooke's thighs and picked gently at the fabric of her skirt while their guests argued over which dish they had enjoyed the most. Andy didn't even feel an urge to get up and start clearing trash, not wanting to break this contact with Brooke. Brooke shifted in the chair. Andy slipped her hand a little farther up Brooke's thigh and was surprised by such a rush of wanting, she almost climbed into Brooke's lap right in front of everyone.

Andy rarely entertained guests, and never before on a holiday. For all the pain she had experienced as a child, Andy had never lost a deep love of society's rituals. She had listened to school friends talk about their family traditions like other kids read fairy tales. They may have dreamed of castles and knights, but she'd longed for a home to be her sanctuary. Brooke had given Andy her fantasy this evening. Andy knew that if she had tried to have this same party without Brooke it wouldn't have been as easy or relaxing. She was the one who had cooked and planned, who had approached the night with a relaxed and generous attitude. She had interacted with Andy's friends as if she had known them for years, making each one feel special and welcome. Andy felt a deep sense of gratitude for Brooke's gift. And a growing desire for her.

And love. Her hand froze as she realized how much she had grown to love Brooke. In every important way, Andy thought of Brooke as a partner. From daily activities to important events, everything Andy did had more depth, more richness, simply because Brooke was there. Over the past few weeks, with Brooke around, her apartment had felt more like home than any place ever had. But it wasn't just the companionship and cooking that made that happen, it was Brooke herself. But what if Brooke went away? Andy didn't know how she would survive.

"Anyone for pumpkin pie?" Brooke asked, bringing Andy back from her thoughts with a start. Every person perked up from their food coma and asked for a piece. Brooke grabbed Andy's hand and stood up. "Come help me?"

"I'll help you," Tina said, waving Andy back into a seated position. "If we leave the two of you in the kitchen with a can of whipped cream, we'll never get dessert."

Andy flushed but everyone else, Brooke included, just laughed. She tried to focus on the conversation and keep her mind away from thoughts of love, or Brooke covered in whipped cream. The homemade pie was a huge hit with everyone, but Andy barely tasted it as she worried about her feelings for Brooke. As soon as she was finished, she started gathering plates and empty glasses, trying to ignore the concerned glances Brooke was sending her way. She carried a stack of plates into the kitchen and tossed them into the garbage and recycle bins under the sink. She sensed Brooke behind her before she turned around.

"What is it?" Brooke asked with a slight frown. "What went wrong?"

Andy shook her head, not knowing how to explain. "It's just been such a great evening," she said quietly. "I'm sorry it's almost over."

Brooke stepped toward her and wrapped her arms around Andy's waist, her chin resting on Andy's shoulder. Andy hesitated before she returned the embrace, longing for the familiar feeling of simple desire instead of this overwhelming rush of love. She pushed Brooke away gently. She had been so careful of their physical relationship and had fought so hard to resist Brooke's body, she hadn't noticed the attack on her heart.

"Thank you for tonight," she said as she took a step back. "You made it perfect for everyone."

Tina popped her head in the room. "Hey, Andy, everyone wants music. Can I play your violin?"

Andy nodded, glad of an excuse to get out of the kitchen before she made a mess of things and professed her love to Brooke. She and Tina went into the music room to get instruments, and David followed. He carried Andy's keyboard out to the living room and set it up while Tina tuned the rarely used violin.

"Do you mind slumming?" Andy asked Richard as she handed him the less expensive viola she used for teaching. He gave an exaggerated grimace as he took the instrument out of its case and slipped on a shoulder rest. He played a few scales, clearly as proficient with this instrument as with the violin.

"It's not *too* bad," he admitted grudgingly as Andy mimicked the scales on her performance viola. The difference in quality between the two instruments was noticeable as the deeper tones from Andy's viola seemed to linger in the air after they were played.

Tina started them off with some fiddle tunes, and the rest of the group joined in when she played "Old Joe Clark." Andy felt her tension easing yet again as their playing deteriorated into a speed contest that had their friends laughing and urging them on. Then David took center stage as the others tried to stump him with a variety of song requests. He could play by ear, so he would pick out the basic melody of any song they asked for, and then the rest of the group joined in.

Andy had played with these people for several years, but she had never spent so much time with them in a social setting. She learned more about them as they played together, and she started to appreciate Richard's subtle sense of humor, Tina's gift for improvising on the violin, and David's perfect pitch. They finished the night with Mozart's "Eine Kleine Nachtmusik," one of Andy's favorites.

"Well-played," Richard complimented her when they finished.

"She should play that one well," Brooke said. "She has it tattooed on her ass."

That silenced everyone as they turned toward her. "I do not," Andy said with a laugh, jabbing at Brooke with her bow. "It's on my lower back."

They wouldn't let her off the hook, so she had to show everyone her tattoo. *I guess they're learning new things about me too,* she thought.

After the music, their guests started to drift toward the door in the usual lengthy process of gathering coats, packing plates of leftovers, and saying good-bye. Finally the two of them were alone in the suddenly very quiet apartment, a moment Andy had been both dreading and anticipating. Andy wanted the physical contact she and Brooke had shared all evening to continue, but they had fallen into the habit, usually enforced by her, of stopping after a brief kiss or touch. Andy was all too aware of her desire, of her jumbled thoughts of love and partnership, but she had no idea what Brooke would expect tonight.

"That was exhausting, but fun," Brooke announced as they surveyed the mess in the living room. "Do you mind if I take a quick shower before we start to clean up?"

"Take your time," Andy said. "I thought I'd call Amy and make sure everything went okay tonight."

Brooke disappeared, and Andy dialed Amy's number. She realized guiltily that she had barely thought about her family all night except to compare their usual holidays with this special one.

She hoped the evening hadn't been too much of a disaster without her there as a buffer.

"Hello?" Amy said brightly when she answered the phone. Her sister was a night owl, so Andy hadn't hesitated to call so late.

"Happy Thanksgiving," she said.

"You, too, sister dear. Did you and the little woman have a good night?"

"I had a nice evening with my friends, thank you," Andy replied without rising to her sister's bait. "How did it go at home?"

"Oh, you know. Same old crap. Dad criticized my clothes and complained that the turkey was dry. Mom kept putting more food on my plate and asking about the possibility of future grandchildren. Just like every other year."

Andy sat heavily in a dining room chair. "Really? No big fights? Everyone was all right?"

"Of course," Amy said with her usual harsh laugh. "What did you expect, the house would come crashing down because you weren't there?"

"No," Andy lied. They floundered around with small talk for a few minutes before hanging up. She set the phone on the table next to a pile of dirty serving dishes and listened to the sounds of Brooke splashing in the shower.

CHAPTER TWENTY

B rooke came out of the bathroom and found Andy at the dining room table. "How is Amy?" she asked anxiously, unable to read Andy's expression. She thought their evening had gone well, but she knew Andy would be consumed by guilt if her fun holiday had come at her family's expense.

Andy shrugged. "She said it was a normal Thanksgiving."

"Well, that's good news," Brooke said with a sigh of relief. "Isn't it?"

"I guess," Andy said, her brow furrowed. "Do you know that feeling you get when you're flying, and you try to concentrate really hard so the plane won't crash? And then you realize you don't really have any control over what happens, so you might as well just sit and enjoy the ride."

No matter how perfect Andy had tried to be, how hard she fought to bring peace to her family, it was always just an illusion. It made Brooke's heart ache to think of how many crashes Andy had survived along the way. "So you discovered that your family won't fall apart if you stop being miserable for one night?" Brooke asked gently.

Andy nodded with a small smile. "It's good to find out, but I wasted a lot of years struggling to keep them together even though they didn't need me to." She met Brooke's eyes. "If it hadn't been for you, I would have gone back this year to the same lousy night. And I would have missed all of this."

She waved her arm vaguely around the room, and when her hand came back to rest on the table Brooke covered it with her own. "Sometimes you need to break out of an old habit before you can see that there are other ways of doing things," Brooke said. They both had needed to separate from their families, if only for a short time, to realize how much of their own identities they sacrificed when they let others define who they should be.

Andy just squeezed Brooke's fingers with her own, staring at their entwined hands. She slipped off her chair and onto her knees in front of Brooke, winding her arms around Brooke's waist and laying her head in her lap. Brooke cupped the back of Andy's head with one hand and rubbed the other gently over her shoulders and upper back. They stayed like that, just resting close to each other, until Andy stopped thinking about her family and started noticing the soft thighs that rested on either side of her rib cage.

"You're wearing my bathrobe," she said quietly, reaching a hand up to play with the robe's belt. "Anything underneath it?"

She felt Brooke's laughter under her cheek. "Do you want to find out?" she asked, bending over to kiss the top of Andy's head.

Andy slid her hand under the loose top of the robe and ran her fingers lightly over Brooke's bare breasts. She raised her head and impatiently untied the loose sash and pushed the robe off Brooke's shoulders. Their eyes locked, and Brooke's were anything but icy as her desire for Andy showed on her face.

"God, you are so beautiful," Andy whispered reverently, running her hands up Brooke's thighs, to her waist, and back to her full breasts. She realized they had been aiming at this moment from the first time they'd touched that afternoon. She gently squeezed Brooke's nipples, and Brooke gripped the back of her head more tightly as she thrust her breasts toward Andy's hungry mouth.

Andy sucked a taut nipple into her mouth, making Brooke gasp with pleasure, while her hands traveled back to the silky legs that enveloped her. She rested her thumbs on the tight tendons at the apex of Brooke's thighs, kneading lightly and loving the response she got as Brooke spread her legs and pressed her hips closer. The smell of Brooke's arousal surrounded her, and she thought she might come just from having Brooke's obvious desire fill all of her senses. Brooke gave a wordless cry of need as Andy's mouth dropped to her wetness and covered her with gentle kisses.

Andy remembered the sweet taste of Brooke, but this time with her was worlds away from their first night together. Then it had been a matter of attraction, of a connection with a beautiful stranger. Now, Andy poured all of her love and gratitude into giving this woman pleasure, and her tongue ran over Brooke with a patient tenderness that drove her wild. Brooke's incoherent cries begged her to move harder and faster, but she refused to be rushed, showing Brooke how much she loved her since she knew she couldn't say the words yet. Andy was determined to make this last, but her slow, deep lovemaking pushed Brooke to an orgasm that shook them both.

"Oh my God," Brooke gasped when she could speak again, tears running down her face. "How did you *do* that?"

She caught Andy's face between her hands and pulled her up for a frantic kiss. Andy leaned her hands on the armrests, bending over Brooke's chair and kissing her with all the passion and need that she had been trying to contain. Their tongues danced, and only the uncomfortable position made Andy finally draw away and help Brooke to her feet. Brooke left the robe lying on the chair, and Andy discarded her clothes as quickly as she could. They fell onto Andy's bed together, tugging at the blankets and sheet to get them out of the way.

"No," Andy whimpered as Brooke started kissing her way down Andy's neck. Brooke raised her head in confusion, but Andy threaded her fingers through silky blond hair and brought her close. "Please, don't stop kissing me."

Brooke smiled and nipped playfully at Andy's lower lip. Andy's tongue snaked out and Brooke met it with her own. Her thigh moved between Andy's legs, and she slid her hand down until she reached wet curls. Andy moved her hips against Brooke's thigh and fingers, letting Brooke fill her mouth with her tongue until she came, crying Brooke's name loudly.

Brooke lifted her head slightly and looked into Andy's eyes, sharing the same breath as they stared at each other in wonder. Andy lifted a shaky hand to brush Brooke's hair from her face before kissing her more gently on the lips. Brooke felt small contractions where her hand was still pressed between Andy's thighs, and she was reluctant to break their contact. Being together now was so different from their first night, when they were strangers and Brooke had been looking for an escape, a fantasy. Now it was real life. Two people who shared meals and shopping trips and household chores, and now shared a bed. The situation was mundane, so much less exciting than picking up a stranger in a bar, but Brooke was overwhelmed by the powerful feelings she experienced. The first time, Andy had touched her body and showed her how amazing sex could be. This time, she'd reached in and touched Brooke's soul.

"Andy, I need you again," Brooke whispered. "Please."

Andy rolled them over and slipped between Brooke's wet thighs. "My pleasure," she growled as she moved lower.

"Faster this time," Brooke panted as Andy seemed intent on maintaining her slow, loving pace. "I don't know if I can take that again so soon, what you did out there."

Andy laughed and caught Brooke firmly with her mouth, sucking around her clit before diving deeply inside with her tongue. "Is that how you want it?" she asked, raising her head to catch Brooke's eye.

"Yes, please." Brooke said.

"Okay, but I just want to make sure I'm doing this right…"

Brooke gave a strangled laugh at Andy's teasing. "Don't stop," she said, kicking gently at Andy with her ankle. Andy grinned at her and returned to business, sliding her fingers inside while her tongue swirled toward Brooke's swollen clit. Brooke thought her first orgasm should have finished her off for the night, leaving her unconscious until morning, but instead it had left her with a driving need to be near Andy. She clenched her fingers in Andy's hair, desperately pulling her closer. This time, Andy's pace matched her need, and soon she was sucking her clit deep into her mouth until Brooke thrust her hips against Andy and came with a loud cry.

Andy moved back up the bed and took Brooke into her arms, holding her tightly as their heads settled close together on Andy's pillow.

"Can I?" Brooke asked in a drowsy voice, her hand drifting down Andy's abdomen.

"Later, honey," Andy whispered, stopping Brooke's hand and tucking it securely around her waist. "Just go to sleep."

❖

Andy woke up the next morning to find Brooke sprawled across the bed, her head pillowed on Andy's stomach and the sheets tangled around their legs.

God, she even sleeps like a slob, Andy thought with affection as she gently threaded her fingers through Brooke's hair, letting the strands drop against her stomach with a feather's touch.

Brooke stretched her arm over Andy's thighs and turned her face, trailing soft kisses over Andy's lower abdomen.

"Good morning," Brooke said. Andy felt her muscles clench as Brooke rubbed her thigh, and she fought to keep her hips from straining toward Brooke's hand.

"We should get out of bed so you can have your coffee," Andy said reluctantly. "And we have one hell of a mess to clean up."

Her sentence ended with a short gasp as Brooke's fingers found her wet and ready to be touched. "In a minute," Brooke suggested, lazily trailing her hand through Andy's wetness. "And last night was worth all the dirty dishes, wasn't it?"

Andy murmured her agreement, focused mainly on Brooke's movements as she slipped between Andy's legs. "We should do the same thing for Christmas. Even if Nancy has the baby before, she won't be able to travel that soon."

Andy's hand rested on Brooke's head and she could feel Brooke still. "Maybe," Brooke said. She went back to kissing her way up Andy's thigh, but Andy suddenly shifted her hips out of Brooke's reach and sat up in bed.

"What do you mean maybe?" Andy asked, her voice hardening as she shut down the arousal that had been her sole focus only moments before. She was suddenly torn back to their first time, waking up alone after Brooke's panicked flight from her bed. She had thought her heart was breaking when the Brooke who had been a stranger left her. How much more would it hurt now after she had been foolish enough to fall in love?

Brooke frowned. "I just don't know what I'll be doing at Christmas. The fuss over my wedding will have died down, so I might be ready to be back with my family."

"You might not really want to be with me, you mean," Andy said, getting out of bed and pulling on the first items of clothing she could find. She was angry with herself for letting Brooke lead her on when clearly all she wanted was a fling. And she was angry at Brooke for not having enough respect for her to be honest about her feelings. She might be inexperienced as a lesbian, but she wasn't ignorant as a woman, or as a friend.

Brooke shook her head, but she didn't deny the truth of Andy's words. "You promised me," she said quietly. "You said I could have until Christmas to decide."

Andy simply stared at her before stalking into the bathroom and slamming the door. Last night had been a promise in her mind. A promise to love and care for this woman. If Brooke hadn't felt that too, then maybe it was better for her to leave. Andy spent most of her shower convincing herself she really believed that, and the rest of it calling herself a fool. She had gotten too close, and she had been stupid. She knew the old story. She was Brooke's first, her experiment. And now she would go on to explore her sexuality, beyond Andy's reach. Go on to build a new life without Andy in it. Andy had read too much into the relationship, and she would be the one to suffer.

❖

Brooke made their morning lattes and left Andy's on the counter, trying not to feel too hurt when Andy simply dumped it down the drain and washed the mug. It was as if she had sucked all of her pain and anger inside and left an Andy-sized chasm in the apartment. Brooke would even have preferred a screaming fight over this deep silence. At least then she might have been able to admit the truth behind her reluctance to make plans for Christmas. The truth about how scared she had been last night by the depth of her feelings for Andy. While Brooke had been trying to give herself space and keep her distance, she had somehow grown powerfully attached to Andy. If such intense feelings could sneak up when she was unaware of them, what would happen if she committed fully to a relationship with her? How could she keep her identity separate when Andy could exert such an influence over her?

They spent an hour cleaning the apartment, somehow managing to spend as little time in the same room as possible. Afterward, Andy simply took her coat and left without a word, skipping her usual practice. Alone and sad, Brooke gathered the clothes Andy had hidden in her closet the day before and tidied them into a corner of the living room, trying to make her presence felt as little as possible in Andy's space. She debated whether she should simply go, but she hated the thought of leaving without at least saying good-bye.

She was eating a lunch of leftovers when Andy finally returned. She shut herself into her bedroom without acknowledging Brooke, and it took her a few minutes to work up the courage to knock on the closed door. There was no answer, as she had expected, but she pushed in anyway.

Andy was lying on her bed, one arm draped over her eyes. "Did I say come in?"

Brooke sat on the bed next to her. "No, but we need to talk."

Andy didn't speak, so Brooke tugged at her arm. "Look at me, please?" When Andy did, Brooke almost regretted having asked. Even in her angry withdrawal, her expressive hazel eyes revealed the depth of her pain.

Brooke took a deep breath and pushed on. "That night of the concert, after you were with Lyssa, you made me a promise. You said no matter how unreasonable I was, you would give me until Christmas to decide."

She knew it was a dirty trick to bring up Andy's guilt-ridden night with Lyssa, but she was desperate. "Are you going to keep that promise, or do you want me to leave?"

"That's not fair," Andy said, her eyes reddening with unshed tears.

"You decide. You can let me stay while I work things out in my head, or you can ask me to go."

"I promised, so you can stay," Andy said through clenched teeth. "But get out of my room."

She covered her eyes again, and Brooke reached out a hand to touch her but stopped short of doing so. She left the room and quietly closed the door.

CHAPTER TWENTY-ONE

Brooke was making a chili and cornbread casserole for dinner when Andy finished her morning practice. She moved to the side so Andy could wash her mug at the sink, neither one speaking as they tried not to bump into each other in the small space.

"Are you almost finished with that?" Andy asked testily, crossing her arms as she leaned on the counter and watched Brooke spooning the cornmeal mixture over the chili.

"Am I in your way?" Brooke snapped.

"No," Andy answered. "Christ, I just thought we could go for a walk. I'm not trying to pick a fight."

"Oh," Brooke stared at the casserole as she put more care than was really required into smoothing the top layer. "A walk. That sounds nice."

She covered the dish and put it in the fridge before taking some warmer clothes into the bathroom so she could change there while Andy shut herself in her bedroom to do the same thing. Brooke brushed her hair and tried to cover the dark smudges under her eyes with some concealer. She hadn't been sleeping well since their fight, and from the look on Andy's face, she hadn't either. She missed Andy's friendship and longed to return to the peace they had known before their all-too-arousing, and terrifying, night together. They met in the hall, and Andy set off without another word.

Brooke gamely tried to keep up with Andy's long strides without breaking into a jog as they marched along the familiar streets, but by the time they reached Broadway's retail area she was cranky and breathing hard.

"Can I at least get some coffee?" she asked, stopping by an espresso stand.

Andy walked on a few yards then circled back when she realized Brooke wasn't following. "No. We don't have time."

"Why are you being so mysterious?" Brooke asked suspiciously. "Is this another therapy setup? Or are we going to meet a hit man?"

Andy rolled her eyes. "If I were hiring a hit man, I wouldn't bring you with me. Just come on," she said, grabbing a reluctant Brooke's hand and pulling her along.

At least Andy slowed her pace slightly so Brooke didn't have to fight to keep up. She let her hand remain in Andy's grasp for almost a block before gently releasing the contact. Even when they were bickering on the street, she still craved Andy's touch. That realization just made her more irritated, and she punched Andy in the arm.

Andy swung to face her, her arms spread wide and an exaggerated questioning look on her face. "What was that for?"

"I'm mad at you," Brooke snapped, walking ahead in rapid strides so it was Andy's turn to play catch-up.

"Well, the feeling's mutual," Andy muttered as they left the shops and restaurants behind and continued along Broadway. They walked in silence until Andy turned off the main sidewalk.

"We're going to school?" Brooke asked as they passed a sign for the Seattle Central Community College. Andy simply shrugged and led them into one of the buildings.

"May I help you?" the young man at the reception desk asked as they approached.

"My friend here has an appointment with the director of the Culinary Arts program," Andy said.

"You must be Brooke Stanton," he said, and Brooke managed a nod. "I'll let her know you're here. You can look through these while you wait," he offered, handing Brooke several brochures.

Andy led the way to a small cluster of chairs and dropped into one. Brooke followed slowly, flipping through the glossy brochures.

"Cooking school?"

"I just thought you might enjoy it," Andy said. "You have a talent for combining flavors, and it seems to make you happy."

Brooke sat on the edge of a chair next to Andy. "How long have you been thinking about this?" she asked, keeping her tone neutral.

Andy shrugged. "Since Thanksgiving. You're so passionate about cooking. I thought it would be a good career to explore."

"So you explored it for me."

"No," Andy said slowly. "I just looked up some local schools, and this seemed like a good program."

Brooke wanted to shred the brochures she held, but she tried to stay calm. She couldn't stop the memory of her dad and Jake telling her she should be a paralegal, listing all the reasons they thought it was perfect for her. "Did it ever occur to you to talk to me about it before you made up your mind?"

"You've barely spoken to me since Thanksgiving, so I didn't have a chance to bring it up," Andy said in a clipped voice. "If you don't want to do it, then don't."

"Whether I like the idea or not isn't the point," Brooke said in frustration. She wasn't sure if she was more furious because Andy kept trying to control her life, or because she seemed so unaware of what she was doing. Even though Brooke felt a thrill of anticipation to learn about this school, she mainly felt a fierce need to protect herself. Her ties to her family and Jake had been strong enough to give them too much control over her life, her decisions. She hadn't thought it possible, but her feelings for Andy threatened to eclipse them all. How would she be able to withstand Andy's influence, without losing her identity completely?

"Then what is the point, Brooke?"Andy asked. "It's not like I signed you up for classes, only a stupid interview."

"Just like you arranged for me to meet Jonas."

"Well, okay. Let's bring that up again," Andy said, leaning back in her chair and crossing her arms. "I thought we had moved past it, but apparently not."

"And I thought you had learned not to go behind my back and try to run my life."

"I'm not…" Andy growled and dropped her head into her hands. She sat up again, and her voice was calmer when she spoke. "We're arguing in circles, Brooke. Let's just get out of here and forget this happened."

"No," Brooke said, feeling dangerously close to shouting. "Because it will happen again. You can't stop yourself from controlling your life, your family, me. I can't take it anymore."

"What do you mean?" Andy said, her voice flat. Brooke opened her mouth to speak, but she was interrupted.

"You can go on back now," the young man called to her. "Second door on the left."

Brooke stood up. "Don't wait for me, Andy," she said, struggling for composure. She'd rather not break down and sob during her interview. "I'll see you at your apartment."

❖

Andy's anger slowly dissipated as she walked home alone. It was obvious Brooke didn't want a relationship with her, not in the way Andy had hoped. Although she would have preferred to simply leave for her evening rehearsal and avoid another confrontation with Brooke, Andy made herself wait so they could finally finish what they had started. She was calmly gathering her music together when Brooke returned.

When she heard the apartment door open, she left her music room and found Brooke in the hall, holding a large manila folder to her chest.

"I have to leave, Andy," she said simply.

Andy nodded. She had been expecting this, especially after Brooke's final words at the school, delivered with such deadly calm. "I'm sorry, Brooke," she said, her own voice emotionless. "I wanted to surprise you with this idea, but I was wrong. And I'm sorry you can't tell the difference between someone who wants to share your life and someone who wants to control it. Between someone who wants to help you discover your passions and someone who dictates what they should be."

"You don't know where the line is yourself," Brooke said. "You make a decision, even with the best of intentions, and then you try to force it on me. I'm scared of…"

Brooke paused, and Andy raised her hands in frustration. "Of what, Brooke?"

"Of you. Of losing myself in you. Of having you take over my life so I can't tell where your decisions leave off and mine begin."

"All you have to say is no, and I'll back off every time," Andy said. How could Brooke believe she'd do anything less? And she couldn't help who she was, either. She made plans, set goals, listed action steps. She should have consulted with Brooke along the way, but why not take care of some of the details first?

"When you care about someone you want to be part of their life," Andy continued. "Not a dictator, and not an observer. Maybe what you're really scared of is finding a job, or a woman, you really care about. Because then you'll need to commit, be an adult, without using your indecision as a crutch to keep you from growing up and taking charge of your own life."

Brooke took a step back as if she'd been slapped. "I know I haven't reached your level of perfection, Andy, but I've been making tough decisions since we met," Brooke said in a quiet, but steady voice. "The hardest so far is saying good-bye to you."

Andy watched until Brooke shut the apartment door behind her, and then she returned to her music room, the one place where focus and hard work were all she required to maintain control. If she could only concentrate hard enough, she'd be able to convince herself that the empty silence in the apartment was peace and the ache inside was merely relief at the abrupt return of her solitary equilibrium. It wouldn't be easy—it never was—but it was the best she could do.

CHAPTER TWENTY-TWO

B rooke woke in the morning lying on her old purple bedspread and stared at the ceiling of her childhood room. She felt disgusted and angry. She had returned to her parents' home the night before with only vague explanations for her sudden presence. She knew they expected more than her cranky excuses, but she had been so angry over Andy's treachery. If she had started talking when she had too little control over her emotions, she would most likely have revealed her feelings for Andy. She hadn't wanted to come out to her parents as a by-product of their fight. Other than an abrupt refusal when her mom suggested she call Jake, Brooke hardly spoke as they moved her boxes, hastily packed when she knew Andy would be out of the apartment at her scheduled rehearsal, into her old room. She had claimed a headache, not entirely fictitious, and shut herself away for the night.

Andy had accused her of refusing to grow up, and Brooke had proved her right by running home to her parents and hiding under the covers. After all the drama and defiance over her cancelled wedding, her insistence on starting a new life on her own terms, she had instead come in a full, miserable circle. She had locked herself in her room like a moody adolescent, complete with whiny tantrum. After all of her efforts to change, she was back on her bed like a confused teenager.

But not confused about everything, she admitted silently. If her time with Andy had given her anything, it was a clear answer about being a lesbian. Brooke didn't know whether their relationship had a chance, and she still fumed over the last ambush, but she knew without a doubt her sexuality was a constant. Her parents deserved to know that much at least.

No, Brooke thought, sitting up in bed, *I deserve to tell them, so I won't have to hide anymore.* Maybe she hadn't taken a leap backward, but instead had come home so she could find enough courage to resolve some of the lies she had been telling in order to please her family. Then she could move forward, free of the past. No more hiding a relationship, whether it was with Andy or someone new. No more hiding behind her equivocation when she was very aware how her body responded to a woman's touch. To *Andy's* touch. Brooke got out of bed and searched for something nice to wear. She clung to her anger from yesterday, using it to drive thoughts of Thanksgiving night from her mind.

Brooke found her parents at the dining room table, drinking coffee in silence. She stood in the doorway and cleared her throat.

"Good morning," she said when they turned to face her.

"Good morning, dear," Evelyn said. "Can I make you some pancakes?"

Brooke had to laugh at her mom's attempt to make the situation seem normal. She almost expected her to ask if Brooke had finished her homework. "I thought we could go out for breakfast," Brooke said. "We should talk."

Her mom looked ready to protest, but Bill spoke up first. "Any place special in mind?"

Brooke suggested the Orca Room, a new upscale restaurant she had been to once with Jake. On the top floor of a downtown hotel, it had expansive views of Puget Sound and some of the best seafood in Seattle. Brooke didn't care about those things, though. She recalled the tables covered in white linen and set with silver, and a stern-looking, uniformed waitstaff. Brooke hadn't felt overly comfortable eating there, but it seemed the least likely of places for her parents to make a scene. If she could just fill the other tables with her mom's country club friends, she'd be set.

They drove to the restaurant and ordered breakfast, and Brooke could barely swallow, let alone speak. Her earlier determination waned, and she seemed to have lost her voice. She half-listened to her parents' forced attempts at small talk, giving only brief comments when required. She stared out at the Sound, watching a ferry make its leisurely way to Bremerton, and fought a sudden longing to have Andy with her. Not speaking for her, but standing with her for support.

Brooke pulled her gaze away from the view and back to her parents. As infuriating as they could be, she loved them. She didn't know how they would react to her after she told them, and the possibility of being cut out of their lives terrified her. She felt a sudden wave of panic, and a fear she would fail yet again to be honest with them. Tears stung her eyes, and she felt her dad's hand cover her own.

"Talk to us, Brooke," he said gently.

"I think…" Brooke stopped and shook her head. No more thinking, no more maybes. "I'm a lesbian."

The three of them were silent for a few moments. Barely audible classical music and the occasional chink of a fork on china were the only sounds in the restaurant. "It's only natural you're confused after all you've been through, Brooke," Evelyn said, patting her daughter's hand. "When we get home, I'll call Dr. Jeffries, and he can help like he did last time."

"He didn't help me, Mom," Brooke said, trying to keep her rising anger out of her voice. She wanted to explain, not argue. "He made me doubt myself, question my own feelings. I won't let anyone do that again."

"Are you doing this because of that musician?" Evelyn asked after a tense pause.

"Andy and I are…were dating, but I'm not gay because of her. I was attracted to her because I like women."

Evelyn winced at Brooke's statement, but the arrival of a waiter with their food effectively halted all conversation for a moment.

"But you came home again," Bill said once they were alone again. "Since you're not with her anymore…"

"No, Dad, it won't change anything. Andy and I had a little disagreement, but I mainly needed to talk to you both," Brooke said, downplaying their argument. Whether or not she and Andy managed to work things out, they would do it with privacy. "I'm tired of running away instead of standing up for myself and being honest. I did the same thing at Gonzaga, with Jake, and with the two of you." *And with Andy,* Brooke added to herself. But that was different, because Andy knew exactly why she left.

"But you lived with Jake. Weren't the two of you…" Evelyn waved her hand in the air to finish her sentence. Brooke knew it was as close as she'd come to bringing up the topic of sex.

"I tried," Brooke said, keeping her own answer equally vague. "I tried to be what everyone wanted me to be."

"We only wanted you to be happy, Brooke," her dad said with a sigh. "But you've chosen a difficult path."

"It's not a decision I've made. It's who I am," Brooke said firmly, needing her parents to understand, as she finally did, that there were no gray areas here. "You can't change me, but I hope you can accept me."

Bill took his wife's hand and they looked at one another for a moment before he spoke. "We love you, Brooke. We always will."

Brooke felt a wave of relief wash over her, and she blinked back tears again. She had worried about her parents causing a scene, but she was the one getting emotional. She attacked her cooling crab eggs Benedict with a sudden appetite.

"I suppose this means no grandchildren," Evelyn said with a resigned sigh.

Brooke choked on a piece of crab. "There are always options, if I decide I want kids," she said, shaking off a sudden vision of Andy with a child, teaching her to play a tiny viola or helping him organize his stuffed animals by size and color.

"Would you like me to tell people at the firm?" Bill asked. "Or do you want to do it yourself, when you come back?"

"I'm not going back there, Dad," Brooke said, hurrying through her words before she started to apologize or waver in her decision.

"I never really liked it. I'm thinking of going to culinary school. I found out I love to cook, and I'm pretty good at it."

Her parents stopped eating and stared at her. "You get that from me," Evelyn said finally, before returning to her lobster crepes.

"Your mother is an excellent cook," Bill agreed.

"I taught you how, before your dad made partner and we started eating out so often," Evelyn said. "Do you remember?"

Brooke smiled. "I used to sit on the counter and watch. You'd give me things to chop or stir."

"I just couldn't let you add the spices," Evelyn said with a small laugh. "You never did like to measure."

The memory triggered a series of reminiscences from Brooke's childhood, as if the three of them needed to revisit the ties holding them together as a family. Brooke welcomed the change to lighter topics and the sense of relief she felt after her honesty. She finished her breakfast, shutting out the desire to share her accomplishment with Andy.

On the other side of town, Andy stood in front of her open refrigerator and attempted to stir up some enthusiasm for the frozen burrito she had chosen for dinner. She had restocked her freezer and shelves with the convenience foods that had been her staples before Brooke had come along and introduced home-cooked meals into her life. She tossed the burrito into the microwave and was setting the timer when a knock at the door gave her that too familiar feeling of hope.

It wasn't Brooke, but her quartet—plus Jonas—who stood on the landing. "We brought pizza and beer," Tina said, holding up a six-pack of Alaskan Amber. "So you have to let us in."

She didn't so much invite them in as stand staring in surprise while they walked past her. Richard patted her stiffly on the shoulder.

"Nancy wanted to come, but she wasn't feeling well today. She wanted me to tell you she's sorry Brooke left," he said before filing into the living room behind Tina.

David came in last and made a show of prying the door out of Andy's hand so he could shut it. He put his index finger under her chin and pushed her mouth closed. "Stop staring at us like you've never seen friends before," he said.

"How did everyone know?" she asked quietly.

"Jonas talked to Brooke yesterday. He thought you might like some company, so here we are. Now go into the kitchen and toss out whatever is beeping in your microwave."

She went into the kitchen and put the cooked burrito in the fridge. "We need plates and napkins," Tina said from behind her.

"I won't eat pizza, you know," Andy said as she dug through her cupboards, her voice laced with irritation because she felt embarrassed that her quartet was talking about her love life.

"We went to Giovanni's down the street so we could get you one with soy cheese," Tina said, unruffled by Andy's grouchiness. "I don't think you can still call it pizza, but it's close."

Andy felt her eyes stupidly well up with tears, and she crossed her arms over her chest. "Why are you doing this?"

"Because we're your friends, Andy. You don't have to face everything alone, you know," Tina explained in a voice that implied that Andy was acting dim.

"But why now? After all these years?"

"We've always been here," Tina said with a shrug. "Maybe you've just been too much in control to notice. But Brooke made you let us into your life, and we're not going anywhere."

Andy couldn't help but wince when Brooke's name was mentioned. "If you want, I can make the guys leave," Tina offered in a low voice. "If you're more in the mood for girl talk, or if you want to cry on my shoulder."

"God, no crying," Andy said with a short laugh. "I will take one of those beers, though."

❖

It was impossible for Andy to remain uptight for long with the laughter and joking around her. The group sprawled around the living room, their coats draped over the back of her couch, eating too much pizza and talking about anything but Brooke. As usual, the talk soon turned to music, and the group shared stories about their interests outside of the classical world. Tina performed regularly at fiddle festivals while David played with a jazz trio. Richard finally admitted he played lead guitar in a rock band with other faculty members from his college. David was begging to be allowed at one of their rehearsals when Andy started gathering their empty pizza boxes.

"I need to take these to the recycling bin outside," she said quietly to Jonas. "Can you come with me?"

He set down his beer and followed her out. They shut the door on Tina and David's laughter and walked down the stairs.

"How is she?" Andy finally managed to ask.

"She's fine," Jonas said. Andy opened her mouth to ask more, but he held up a hand. "Don't, Andy. Even though she isn't technically my patient, I have to protect her privacy."

They stood by the blue bin, listening to the rain hit the roof of the carport. Andy rubbed her arms, but more because she felt exposed than because she noticed the cold and damp.

"By the way, your apartment looks great," Jonas said casually. "Very clean. And I noticed you've moved the furniture since Thanksgiving."

Andy wouldn't meet his eyes. "I just moved everything back the way it was…before."

"Well, it must feel good to have order restored," he said with a nod. "No more tripping over someone else's clothes and shoes, or juggling for space in the bathroom."

"I like things to be neat," Andy said, not convincingly.

"Under control."

"Exactly."

Jonas laughed. "I'll bet you've even planned your days down to the minute. When to practice, when to eat, like that."

Andy blushed, thinking of the schedule she had posted just yesterday morning in her music room. It was supposed to help her keep her mind on task and off Brooke. She managed to do that during most of her practice time and the fifteen minutes it took to microwave and eat a veggie burger or can of soup. But when she was in the car or teaching or lying in bed, her mind drifted to honey-blond hair sifting through her fingers or the feel of Brooke's skin against her own.

"Those people upstairs love you, Andy," Jonas said, interrupting her thoughts. "But do you know why they've never dropped by your apartment like this before?"

"I guess I don't share much of myself with other people. I like to handle things on my own, and I don't see what's wrong with that."

"Nothing at all," Jonas said. "But it can be a lonely road. Brooke changed you. She made you more approachable, more open, and the people who want to be your friends could feel that."

"But look what happened," Andy said, running a hand through her hair. "I let her in and she hurt me."

"And look what happened to *her*. She got close to you, and it scared her. You can be a lot to live up to, Andy," he said, holding her arm so she would stay and listen. "You're a gifted musician, organized, focused. And that can be intimidating to someone who is spontaneous, a little untidy, and just starting to learn about herself."

"So I practice an instrument and clean my apartment now and then," Andy said with a catch in her voice, both angry and embarrassed at Jonas's words. "I never wanted to make her feel like she's less than I am."

"You didn't," Jonas said, pulling her into a gentle hug. "You made her feel capable of more than she thought she could be. You've spent a lifetime being self-sufficient and in charge of yourself. She's only had a couple of months."

"I miss her," Andy admitted. "But I'm still angry."

"I know," Jonas said, stepping back and meeting Andy's eyes. "I can tell you she misses you too. But she's still confused and needs to find her way and make serious choices. And she's still angry because you didn't trust her to do those things on her own."

They walked back to the apartment in silence. Andy said good night to her friends, appreciating their gesture that evening. But she wasn't convinced by Jonas's words. Yes, Brooke had made her more open, but that had only led to heartbreak. Her old way of life, self-contained and orderly, offered predictability and safety. She quickly tidied the living room, removing all signs of the impromptu pizza party. She retreated into her music room, practicing nothing but scales for the hour before her schedule told her it was bedtime.

CHAPTER TWENTY-THREE

Brooke spent the week trying gamely to be what Jonas called "productively sad" instead of withdrawing as she had in the past. She had gone to his office the day after coming out to her parents, on the pretense of dropping off some completed transcriptions, and ended up spending his lunch hour talking about her family, and about Andy.

"Give her a few days to cool off," he had advised. "And to miss you."

Brooke wanted to talk to Andy, to find out if they could at least remain friends, but she needed to mend old relationships first. She spent time with her parents, and she found she was able to voice her own ideas on any topic more easily since their breakfast. Her mom was clearly uncomfortable, still unable to come to terms with her revelation, but she no longer brought up Dr. Jeffries, so Brooke was happy enough. Her dad was the one to surprise Brooke, though. He didn't claim to understand her feelings for Andy, but he seemed to grow more proud of Brooke every time she asserted herself or expressed her own opinions. They started to enjoy simply spending time together, as they had when she was a child, and he would join her on shopping trips or on walks around the city. Brooke commandeered the barely used kitchen as a way of occupying her time, and she soon had her parents' freezer stocked with food.

Meanwhile, she applied for cooking school and student loans, planning to take on extra transcription work so she could aim toward an independence she hadn't experienced before. She even found some time to be alone, something she'd had very little of in her old life. Since leaving college, she'd rarely been away from Jake, her family, her coworkers—until Andy. Although she had felt lonely at first when Andy was practicing or teaching, she had discovered that having time alone to read, cook, or walk had been refreshing.

❖

By Friday, however, she had been alone and productive enough. She knew she had to see Andy before her big concert, and she hoped her anger had eased, so they could talk and try to work things out. This performance meant so much to Andy. Brooke knew firsthand how much time Andy had put into her preparation, and she wanted to share in her triumph, even if it was only as her friend. She dressed with care, choosing a new navy silk top with a lacy camisole peeking out that she knew Andy would love, and headed down to Pioneer Square. She would check at Mickey's first, to see if the musicians had gone there after their rehearsal. If not, then she would go to Andy's apartment.

She had to circle the surrounding blocks several times in search of a parking place, and she felt a thrill of nervousness when she saw Andy's car near the bar. Mickey's was jammed, and she stood just inside the door and scanned the crowds for the musicians from the symphony. She finally found them, a group of ten people clustered around a small table in the back of the room. She spotted Andy in their midst, breathtaking in black jeans and a turtleneck, leaning close to a woman Brooke didn't recognize. The other woman looked to be in her mid-forties, with short graying hair and elegant features, and she wore a dark maroon jacket and black pants. She was gesturing as she talked to Andy, both of their faces intent on the conversation.

Brooke wiped suddenly sweaty palms on her jeans and headed to the bar to order a drink before confronting Andy. She leaned against the counter, staring at Andy as she waited for the bartender to notice her, but a familiar voice from behind broke her out of her trance.

"They make a handsome couple, don't they?"

Brooke turned to find Lyssa standing close beside her. "Who?" she asked.

Lyssa just smiled. "That's Adrienne Richman, the guest conductor for tomorrow night's concert. She and Andy have been inseparable this week."

The bartender came by, but Brooke waved him away. "So she's not from around here?" she asked hopefully.

"She's with the Chicago Symphony. She also is one of the leading producers of recordings by women composers. You know how important Andy thinks it is to get female musicians the recognition they deserve, and those two have discovered quite a bond."

Brooke glanced over her shoulder and saw Andy laugh at something Adrienne said. She looked happy and in her element. Sharing her ideas and passions with another music expert, and not missing Brooke at all.

"I've heard that Adrienne's principal violist may be leaving, so they'll be holding a national audition for the chair. I wouldn't be surprised if Chicago found itself with a new viola player next season, especially if Andy doesn't keep the first chair here," Lyssa mused, taking a sip of her cosmo and watching the two musicians. She looked back at Brooke. "Why don't you come over and say hi to everyone?"

"No...I can't," Brooke stammered. "I mean, I really need to get going."

Lyssa raised her glass in a silent good-bye, and Brooke left the bar without a backward glance.

Brooke was in her parents' kitchen after midnight, the granite countertops covered with her usual mess of ingredients and utensils. She hadn't been able to sleep since finding Andy with another woman, so she came downstairs to cook. Her dad had been dropping hints all week for chocolate mousse, so she decided to make his favorite dessert instead of tossing in bed.

She cracked eggs against the bowl's edge with more force than necessary and blinked away the threat of tears. She wouldn't cry over Andy, not anymore. Well, at least not tonight. Brooke was the one who had walked away, leaving Andy free to find someone new. *She could've waited more than a week to do it, though,* Brooke fumed as she fished some bits of broken shell out of her egg yolks.

Brooke turned a hand mixer on high and attacked the bowl of eggs and sugar. Brooke cared about Andy, she wanted her to be happy. Just not with someone else. She wished she could erase the picture of Andy with the elegant Adrienne from her mind, but everywhere she looked she saw them leaning close and laughing together. To be fair, they hadn't been sitting any closer than normal for two people carrying on a conversation in a crowded bar. And they weren't touching. Brooke watched the eggs change color and texture, her cheeks flaming, as she recalled the night she and Andy had met at Mickey's. There had probably been no doubt in anyone's mind where they were headed after they left the bar. The only evidence Brooke had to prove Andy and Adrienne were a couple came from Lyssa. Brooke switched off the mixer and wiped some splatters off the counter. She could almost hear her father's voice, warning her not to reach conclusions based on the testimony of a hostile witness.

Her dad and Andy would probably get along well, Brooke decided as she set a pan of chocolate to melt on the glass stovetop. Andy was a lot like him. Irritatingly logical and in control. *But never fickle,* Brooke thought with conviction as she took the chocolate off the stove and idly stirred while it cooled. Maybe she had let Lyssa plant doubt in her mind about Andy's faithfulness, but there was no denying a woman like Adrienne would be perfect for her. Someone talented and successful, confident and sexually self-assured. Not a woman whose life was still filled with question marks. Brooke sighed. She wasn't sure which hurt worse. To believe Andy was involved with someone besides her, or to believe she should be.

Her own words echoed in her mind as she poured a dark ribbon of chocolate into the eggs. Andy should be with someone like

Adrienne. She turned the mixer on again, to a lower setting this time so she didn't decorate the kitchen any more than she already had, and started to blend. The new Brooke fought anyone who attempted to tell her what to feel or think, but wasn't she doing the same thing now, deciding who Andy ought to care for? Because she knew the truth. She knew Andy cared for her, she had seen plenty of proof of Andy's feelings over the past months.

Brooke's dad had pushed her toward Jake because he thought it would make her happy. Andy had pushed her toward culinary school for the same reason. But her father didn't seem to love her any less because she had made a different decision. In fact, he seemed to respect her more when she chose to stand up for her own needs, and their relationship had grown stronger as she had become more independent. And Andy had never tried to force her own passions on Brooke. She hadn't tried to make her musical or compulsively neat. Instead, she had looked at Brooke, at what made *her* happy, and tried to offer it to Brooke in her own ungainly way. Brooke dumped a bowl of whipped cream into the chocolate and started to fold them together, stirring until the marbled mixture was smoothly blended. She sat on the kitchen stool with a spoon, just to taste, and contemplated her next move. She wanted to go see Andy now, to talk to her, but she didn't want to drop by so late. She wasn't sure if she was more concerned about disturbing Andy's sleep the night before her concert or about maybe finding Adrienne in her apartment. Tomorrow would have to be soon enough.

Andy unlocked her apartment door and flipped on the light. It had been difficult to come home all week knowing Brooke wasn't going to be there, but she felt a little less pain than usual tonight. The final rehearsal for the Clarke sonata had gone well, and she had actually enjoyed herself at Mickey's afterward. The guest conductor from Chicago had been fascinating company, and their shared interest in music and women composers had given them plenty to talk about.

It had been a comfortable conversation, for the most part, and it helped to keep Andy from dwelling on Brooke. Thoughts of her were never far away, but at least they hadn't been at the forefront of Andy's mind all night. Except when Andy looked at the table where they had shared their first kiss. Or when she recalled the feel of Brooke's fingers slipping across her stomach and into her waistband as she'd pulled her closer at the bar. Andy opened the fridge to get a beer, but changed her mind and took out a bottle of Chianti instead, as if to torture herself even more. She remembered shopping with Brooke the day they bought the wine, planning a meal that was never made because Brooke left only days later. Andy opened a drawer and found the corkscrew neatly in its place beside a paring knife. She sighed as she pulled out the cork. She could have found it in the dark. When Brooke was here, it usually took fifteen minutes of rummaging to find any utensil since she seemed incapable of putting anything back where it belonged.

Andy sat on the sofa with her glass of wine and looked around the living room. Everything was tidy and the surfaces bare in an attempt to erase any sign of Brooke from her life, but to Andy's eyes the room was still cluttered with ghosts of Brooke and her rampant belongings no matter how much she cleaned. Her apartment had been neat before Brooke arrived, but now it was positively sterile.

Like her life, Andy admitted. Without Brooke, she was back to her usual routine of practice and teaching, but now she noticed all of the empty spaces. She had created a bare outline of a life, but Brooke had filled in the gaps with laughter and shared meals, intimacy and mind-blowing sex. Andy finished her wine and set the glass on a coaster. Brooke had brought passion to her world, a passion Adrienne had commented on this evening when she complimented Andy on her interpretation of the second movement of the Clarke sonata. She asked what inspired Andy as she played it, and Andy had surprised herself by mentioning Brooke. She had always thought of the vivace section as Brooke's movement. It was full of fast-paced notes that challenged both the upper and lower ranges of the viola, as if the sonata were struggling to break free from the structure imposed on it. It required more agility in fingering and bowing than usual in the viola repertoire, and Andy felt both thrilled by and frightened of it. Whenever she played it, she played for Brooke.

Andy had started to list the differences between her and Brooke, but Adrienne had waved off her explanations. Instead, she told Andy about her partner, a scientist with little musical knowledge, and how they had worked to create a relationship even though they were so different. *She is my counterpoint,* Adrienne had said. *We each face the challenge of accepting another person without trying to change her notes and rhythm to match our own. But, like Bach, once you allow each melodic line to have its own voice, the new harmony that emerges is worth the effort.*

Andy got up and washed her wineglass, putting it neatly in the cupboard. She had wanted to protest and claim she had never tried to change Brooke's unique melody, but she had some doubts. Maybe she had attempted to tweak a note here and there. Brooke had been unsure about her future and her career, and Andy might have pushed her to make decisions she needed to reach on her own. But Brooke's choices threatened to take her out of Andy's life. Was she willing to get close again only to lose Brooke once she found her way? Her life was empty and sterile without Brooke, but it had one benefit. Andy couldn't worry about Brooke leaving if she was already gone.

Chapter Twenty-four

B rooke heard the muffled sounds of Andy fitting in a last-minute practice when she arrived at the apartment, but the music stopped when she rang the doorbell. She found herself trying to assume the distant expression she usually wore when nervous or worried, but she couldn't put that wall up in front of Andy anymore. She twisted her hands together and jumped a foot when Andy finally answered the door. Part of her had hoped Andy would grab her in a welcoming hug, but she clearly had no intention of doing so. Brooke had made Andy wait a long time while she figured out her feelings, and now it was her turn.

"Hi," she said breathlessly, unable to hide her smile when she saw Andy in her usual sweats and baseball shirt. No bra, of course. Brooke clenched her fists to keep from reaching out, her determination to be patient dissolving with Andy so close.

Andy leaned against the door, her face a mask. She simply raised her eyebrows instead of asking why Brooke was there.

"I...I took the bus here from Pike Place," Brooke stammered. "I wanted to see you before tonight. To wish you luck."

"Thanks," Andy said and started to shut the door.

"Don't, please," Brooke said as she pushed her way past Andy and into the hallway. "Just talk to me for five minutes."

Andy sighed and shut the apartment door. "What do you want?" she asked in a more normal voice. It was a start, Brooke decided, so she pressed on.

"How have you been?" she asked. She could see the signs of sleeplessness on Andy's face, and she wondered what Andy had been eating this week without her there to cook.

"Fine," she answered. "And you?"

Brooke shrugged. "The same. I applied to the culinary arts program."

"I'm glad, Brooke, I know you'll do great there. Now I really should get back to my practice."

She tried to herd Brooke toward the door, but stopped at her next words.

"I came out to my parents, Andy. I told them about you."

Andy crossed her arms over her chest and wouldn't meet Brooke's eyes, but Brooke kept talking. "I know I hurt you so many times, and I'm sorry about that. And I know it might be too late to ask you to trust me again, but if there's any way…"

Andy held up a hand to stop her. "I can't survive another morning after, Brooke," she said, pain etched across her face. "I can't let you get close and lose you again."

Brooke shook her head. "You won't, Andy. I've made my choice, and it's you. Can we just talk? Go out for coffee or a walk and start over again?"

Andy shrugged and wiped a hand wearily over her eyes. "I can't deal with this now," she said. "I have to concentrate on the concert. Maybe tomorrow?"

"Tomorrow," Brooke whispered. She wanted to reach out for Andy, but her expression warned Brooke not to get too close yet. "That sounds good."

She walked past Andy to the door. "Do you mind if I come to the concert tonight?"

"I got you a ticket a couple of weeks ago," Andy said with a shrug. "I never cancelled, so it'll be at the box office if you want it."

"Thanks," she said. Andy opened the door for her, and she paused close enough that she could smell Andy's shampoo. "I almost forgot. I brought you these from Pike Place." She handed Andy a sack of cinnamon-sugar mini-doughnuts.

Andy peered in the bag. "I thought these were sold by the half dozen, but there are only three in here," she said suspiciously. "Do you have cinnamon on your breath?"

Brooke gave a half laugh, half sob of relief. That sounded so much like her old Andy that she felt a renewed hope they could work things out. "You tell me," Brooke said and gave her a quick kiss on the mouth. "Now go finish your practice."

Brooke walked away, torn between hope and dejection. Andy said they could talk, but one glance inside her apartment showed Brooke all traces of her presence had been wiped clean. Everything she had moved or touched was spotless and back in its proper place. She wondered if she had waited too long to make her choice, or if Andy might be willing to let Brooke disrupt her home and her life once more.

CHAPTER TWENTY-FIVE

B rooke arrived at the concert with David and Jonas, but separated from them so she could pick up her ticket at will call. She found a note from Andy clipped to the envelope, saying she needed to talk to her before the concert. Brooke showed the note to an usher near the door leading backstage and waited nervously for him to find Andy. She worried that it was a bad sign for Andy to summon her like this in a public place instead of waiting to see her tomorrow. She probably wanted to say they were through for good, Brooke decided, and get it out of the way so she could concentrate on her playing.

Andy finally appeared and pulled Brooke inside the door to an empty hallway as the usher returned to his post. They looked at each other in silence for a moment, the muffled sounds of the concertgoers reaching them through the door.

"I only have a few minutes, but I needed to talk to you," Andy said, taking both of Brooke's hands gently in her own. "I've been trying to figure out exactly how to put this, so can you just let me get it out before you say anything?"

Brooke just nodded mutely. She was afraid she might start crying if she made a sound, so she was glad to let Andy do the talking. She had been expecting the worst, so Andy's first words took her by surprise.

"I love you, Brooke. I have probably since our first night together, but I didn't realize it until Thanksgiving. I felt so close to you, but you still weren't ready. Weren't sure it was me you wanted."

Andy paused. "I expected you to be at the same place, to be as ready to commit as I was. I felt like you were betraying me, but you never did. You never promised more than you gave, and you were always honest about needing until Christmas to decide."

Andy squeezed Brooke's hands and stepped a little closer. "I've made up my mind about us. I want you in my life, and I'm willing to take you on your own terms, not mine. I won't organize your life, and I won't try to force a commitment. You can have until Christmas, or Easter, or five years from now to make a decision if you need the time. No promises, no pressure, okay?"

Brooke barely managed a nod before the door opened and Adrienne came into the hall.

"Good evening, Andrea," she said before smiling at Brooke. "And this must be your muse?"

Andy introduced them while making no move to hide their joined hands. Brooke had been fairly confident in her dismissal of Lyssa's stories, but she didn't mind having her faith in Andy confirmed. "I hate to break into your conversation, but we need to prepare," Adrienne said. "It was a pleasure to meet you, Brooke. I hope you enjoy the concert, and I hope you can hear it when Andrea truly plays for you alone."

"I have to go," Andy said quietly, tucking a strand of Brooke's hair behind her ear. "Will I see you after?"

"I'll be waiting," Brooke whispered, pulling Andy into a tight hug. "Good luck."

Adrienne linked her arm companionably through Andy's as they headed down the hall. Brooke pushed through the door and made her way over to Andy's friends. She saw the other members of the quartet apparently engaged in a heated discussion. Jonas, Nancy, and a woman Brooke guessed was Tina's latest stood to one side and watched the argument.

Jonas came over as she approached.

"You're smiling," he said with an answering grin. "I take it you won't need a ride back home tonight?"

"I hope not," Brooke said. "But I'll have to let you know after the concert."

They walked over to the group. Their brief argument was apparently over, and they had drawn Nancy and Tina's date into their discussion. Brooke listened to the conversation as it jumped rapidly from topic to topic. She had been so focused on her own identity over the past months, she hadn't noticed that Andy was already surrounded by a seemingly incongruous mix of friends.

"So how did Andy get involved with this quartet?" Brooke asked. "You're all so different. I guess I would have expected her to join a group of people more like her."

"Silly Brooke," David said as he put an arm around her shoulders. "Andy didn't join our group, she picked us to join her. She claimed she wanted four unique styles because we'd make the music more interesting, but I think she simply found us too charming to resist."

Andy struggled to focus as Adrienne gathered the soloists together before the concert. The joy of seeing Brooke's smile again, the feel of her in Andy's arms, distracted her from the night ahead. Luckily, Adrienne's words managed to bring her back to the music she was about to play.

"I want to impress upon you the importance of tonight's concert," Adrienne began. "When Amy Beach and Rebecca Clarke were composing, many people thought it was improper for women to write music. There were even people who did not believe they could possibly have written these works without a man's help. And when Ellen Taaffe Zwilich was born in 1939, many large orchestras still wouldn't allow women to join, yet she ended up being the first woman to win a Pulitzer Prize for music. For the very symphony we are playing this evening, as you know."

She paused and looked at the four of them. "You deserve to play these sonatas because you are excellent musicians, not simply because you are women. But when you are onstage, remember that it has often been a battle to give women this opportunity to perform. Be grateful for those who fought for the right to fully express themselves musically, or in any other form. I know you will make me proud tonight, but do not perform for me. Perform for your composers, so that their work will live on."

"Jesus," Andy muttered when Adrienne glided away. "What the hell kind of pep talk was that?"

"I was nervous enough without thinking that I'm playing for all womankind," Joan, Lyssa's pianist, agreed. Even Lyssa looked a little pale after the speech.

Andy jumped when she and Maggie, her pianist, were called to the stage. They stood in the wings waiting for their entrance, and Andy nervously wiped her sweaty palms on her black pants.

"I think I might be sick," she admitted.

"I know," Maggie said. "It's a great feeling, isn't it?"

Andy stared at her and could see that Maggie wasn't being sarcastic. A glow of anticipation lit her face, and Andy felt it spreading to her as well. She was accustomed to a sense of peace when she played her viola in the middle of the section. There was little chance of disaster, as long as she carefully prepared her part and focused during the performance. Small mistakes could be covered up, difficult passages could be fudged if necessary. Now, however, it seemed like every time she had to play, there was more at stake. She was surprised to discover that despite the nausea, Maggie was completely right. It *was* a great feeling.

Andy walked onto the stage and acknowledged the polite applause as she and Maggie took their places. She could feel the audience's expectant hush like a palpable thing. She glanced at Maggie, communicating easily after so many practice sessions, and then launched into the first trumpetlike notes of the sonata. The agitated opening sounds of the first movement helped work off Andy's initial nervousness, and soon she settled into the fluctuating rhythms that she had described to Brooke as a viola having mood swings.

She poured her heart into the second movement, imagining herself in her practice room playing for Brooke who leaned against the door frame watching. The spontaneous burst of applause after the vivace section brought her back to the concert hall and gave her a moment to catch her breath before she launched into the third movement. This section had to be played with strength, showing off the power of the viola through the lyrical passages and into the faster final notes of the sonata. Twenty minutes flew by, and soon she and Maggie had finished and were taking their bows. Applause followed them offstage, and Adrienne hissed at them to play their encore. She had insisted they practice a short Scottish melody of Clarke's, but Andy hadn't expected to need it. She and Maggie sailed easily through the encore, their enjoyment of the simple melody evident in their playing. Finally they left the stage, barely making it to the wings before Adrienne pulled them both into a big hug.

"Beautifully done, my dears," she said before turning her attention to Lyssa and Joan who were about to begin their sonata.

Andy experienced a delayed case of the shakes during Lyssa's flawless solo, and she wanted nothing more than to go find Brooke in the audience. She managed to pull herself together enough to return to the stage with the orchestra and play Zwilich's symphony. She hurriedly put her viola away, accepting the congratulations from various members of the orchestra, and rushed out of the room to find Brooke.

She saw her immediately, standing by the door leading backstage, but she was unprepared for the rest of the crowd. Normally after a concert, she left by the stage door with the other players and headed to her car alone. Tonight, however, she joined the throng of people in the lobby and only managed a wave at a beaming Brooke before she was engulfed by the members of her quartet.

"Very nicely played," Richard said after she gave him and his still hugely pregnant wife a hug. "You conveyed the emotion of the piece, yet still gave a technically sound performance."

"He means you kicked ass," David translated as he and Jonas congratulated her. "I've already started a composition for solo viola in my head. You're the inspiration, so you can be the first to perform it."

Tina gave her a hug as well, a short redhead hovering behind her. "You looked too damned sexy up there," she whispered in Andy's ear. "I think my date is half in love with you."

"Is it finally my turn?" Brooke asked from behind her. Andy turned and felt her heart skip when she saw the look in Brooke's eyes.

"It's always your turn," Andy said and Brooke moved unhesitatingly into her arms, giving Andy a kiss that almost made her drop her viola case.

Brooke reached up a hand to cup Andy's cheek. "You were perfect. I was so proud."

Andy wrapped her in a big hug "I want to come home with you, Andy," Brooke said when she pulled out of Andy's embrace. "Tonight. I brought a suitcase."

"Did you bring the espresso machine?" Andy asked, keeping her voice casual even though her heart was racing.

Brooke laughed. "No, but we can get it tomorrow."

"Well, my apartment has seemed a little too clean lately," she said with a shrug, stepping closer to Brooke. "I guess I wouldn't mind having you mess it up again."

"This calls for a celebration," David said, slapping them both on the back. "Why don't we go to Mickey's for a drink?"

Andy and Brooke stopped kissing long enough to glare at him, but their friends jumped at the invitation.

"One very quick drink," Andy said, her arm wrapped tightly around Brooke's shoulders.

They went to Jonas's car to get Brooke's suitcase. Brooke still held her hand tightly, even as strangers kept stopping Andy to tell her how much they had enjoyed the evening. The attention was flattering but tiring, and all Andy wanted was a chance to be alone with Brooke for a moment at least. She breathed a sigh of relief when they finally were together in her car, Brooke's suitcase stowed in the trunk with Andy's viola.

Andy stuck the key in the ignition, but Brooke covered her hand and stopped her. "I've missed you so much this week," she said, her eyes lowered. "I've been afraid to admit it to myself, or to you, but I love you, Andrea Taylor."

Andy reached over and touched Brooke's chin, turning her head toward her. "Please, Brooke," she whispered, "don't make more promises than you plan to keep. I don't think I can take another night of believing we're in love only to have you change your mind again the next day. I meant what I said earlier. You don't have to say that unless you're sure."

"I am sure," Brooke said, meeting Andy's eyes. The love Andy saw there convinced her more than Brooke's words could.

"I love you too," she said, leaning forward so their lips met. "I love you," she whispered again, against Brooke's mouth.

Their kiss was gentle until Brooke lightly bit at Andy's lower lip, making her open her mouth with a soft sigh. Brooke slipped her tongue into Andy's mouth, deepening the kiss as her hands clenched in Andy's hair. Andy resisted the urge to pull Brooke into her lap, since members of the orchestra were still filtering past the car. They broke away from each other, both breathing deeply.

"We're starting to fog up the windows," Brooke said with a weak laugh. "We should get to the bar, or they'll wonder what's happened to us."

"They know what's happened," Andy said with a grin. Then her expression grew more serious. "I want to go home with you. Now."

"Me too," Brooke agreed, leaning her forehead against Andy's. "But tonight is for you. Let us all show you how happy we are that you did well and how much we love you. I'll be there when we get home."

"And in the morning?" Andy asked, the pain from their last night together still present.

"I promise I will be there in the morning," Brooke whispered with a soft kiss.

Chapter Twenty-six

B rooke!"
    Brooke turned on the burner under a stockpot full of chestnut soup to warm it for Christmas dinner before following Andy's voice into the bedroom. She was digging through a drawer, barefoot and wearing only her black jeans.

"I can't find my green sweater," she said in exasperation. "You have your own dresser, so why are all of your clothes migrating into mine?"

Brooke only sighed and opened the closet. "Wear this instead," she said, handing Andy a dark gold dress shirt. "It brings out the color of your eyes."

"Meaning you have no idea where my sweater is," Andy muttered, reaching for the shirt as Brooke held it just out of reach so that Andy had to step closer.

"It's in the bottom drawer," she said, her eyes roaming over Andy's naked torso. "But I think I prefer what you have on now."

Andy smiled then and pushed gently against Brooke, backing her against the wall next to the closet. She pulled the shirt from Brooke's unresisting hand and tossed it onto the bed behind her.

"How do you do it?" she asked, nuzzling along Brooke's neck, losing herself in the sweet smell of Brooke's hair and skin.

"Do what?" Brooke asked, her question ending in a small gasp as Andy's hand moved under her sweater and caressed her breast.

"Make me forget everything I'm worried about and only think of wanting you," Andy said, raising her head, her vision tunneling until all she saw were Brooke's expressive eyes. She kissed Brooke on the mouth as her right hand reached down and unbuttoned Brooke's jeans.

"We don't have time…" Brooke said, although she made no move to keep Andy from unzipping her pants.

"Quick now, slow later," Andy promised as her hand found its way past Brooke's underwear. She smiled in surprise as her fingers found Brooke slick with moisture. "God, baby, you're so wet already," she murmured into Brooke's ear.

"What have I told you about wearing bras around the house?" Brooke said with a weak laugh, her breath catching as Andy's fingers entered her yielding softness. "You know you drive me crazy when you don't."

"Then I'm throwing them all away," Andy said as her fingers grew bolder in their exploring. "That is, if I can even find them in my dresser."

Brooke arched against her, and Andy slid her left arm around Brooke's waist to help support her. "I've got you, Brooke," Andy whispered. "Let go."

Brooke dropped more of her weight onto Andy's hand, moving her hips and taking Andy's fingers deep inside her. Andy dragged her thumb across Brooke's clitoris, matching the rhythm of her stroking fingers, until Brooke cried out as she climaxed.

She sagged back against the wall, still held up by the strong arm that Andy had wrapped around her. Andy gently brushed Brooke's lower lip with a finger still wet from Brooke's arousal before raising it to her own lips. They kissed as Andy maneuvered them over to the bed and lowered Brooke to a sitting position.

"Do you want your Christmas present now?" Andy asked, pulling on the gold shirt and buttoning it while Brooke leaned back on her elbows and watched.

"You mean there's more?" Brooke asked with a grin.

Andy disappeared into her music room and came back with a small box in red wrapping. She sat next to Brooke and handed her the gift.

"Richard is bringing yours since I didn't have anywhere to hide it," Brooke said as she tore the paper off the present. She knew Andy was going to love the ornate music stand that she had found in an antique shop. Its wood was the same reddish gold as her viola, and it would look much more beautiful than the metal utility stand that Andy used for practice.

"Oh, Andy, I love it!" Brooke exclaimed when she opened the box. She traced the necklace with her finger, admiring the small tiger-head pendant with diamond eyes that dangled from the delicate gold chain. She held her hair out of the way while Andy fastened the necklace around her throat, and then turned to face her. "And I love you."

Andy ran her thumb along the chain that lay across Brooke's collarbone before leaning in for a kiss. "I love you too."

A knock at the door interrupted them, and Andy pulled Brooke to her feet with an impatient sigh. "These holidays are exhausting, and there's no time for us," she said as they returned to the kitchen. They had spent Christmas Eve uncomfortably visiting first Andy's family and then Brooke's parents, and now Andy's quartet was here for Christmas dinner. "Don't even think about inviting everyone for New Year's."

Brooke turned away and stirred her soup.

"You already told them to come over, didn't you?" Andy asked with a laugh.

"Jan's coming to visit us for a few days, and I told you I think she and Tina will hit it off. So I figured we may as well have a party. Now go answer the door because your friends are waiting for you." She turned back to Andy and gave her a quick kiss. "We have the rest of our lives to work on our duet."

About the Author

Karis Walsh is a horseback riding instructor who lives on a small farm in the Pacific Northwest. When she isn't teaching or writing, she enjoys spending time outside with her animals, reading, playing the viola, and riding with friends.

Books Available From Bold Strokes Books

Harmony by Karis Walsh. When Brooke Stanton meets a beautiful musician who threatens the security of her conventional, predetermined future, will she take a chance on finding the harmony only love creates? (978-1-60282-237-5)

nightrise by Nell Stark and Trinity Tam. In the third book in the everafter series, when Valentine Darrow loses her soul, Alexa must cross continents to find a way to save her. (978-1-60282-238-2)

Crush by Lea Santos. Winemaker Beck Montalvo loves a good challenge, but could wildly anti-alcohol, ex-cop Tierney Diaz prove to be the first obstacle Beck can't overcome? (978-1-60282-239-9)

Men of the Mean Streets: Gay Noir edited by Greg Herren and J.M. Redmann. Dark tales of amorality and criminality by some of the top authors of gay mysteries. (978-1-60282-240-5)

Women of the Mean Streets: Lesbian Noir edited by J.M. Redmann and Greg Herren. Murder, mayhem, sex, and danger—these are the stories of the women who dare to tackle the mean streets. (978-1-60282-241-2)

Cool Side of the Pillow by Gill McKnight. Bebe Franklin falls for funeral director Clara Dearheart, but how can she compete with the ghost of Clara's lover—and a love that transcends death and knows no rest? (978-1-60282-633-5)

Firestorm by Radclyffe. Firefighter paramedic Mallory "Ice" James isn't happy when the undisciplined Jac Russo joins her command, but lust isn't something either can control—and they soon discover ice burns as fiercely as flame. (978-1-60282-232-0)

The Best Defense by Carsen Taite. When socialite Aimee Howard hires former homicide detective Skye Keaton to find her missing niece, she vows not to mix business with pleasure, but she soon finds Skye hard to resist. (978-1-60282-233-7)

After the Fall by Robin Summers. When the plague destroys most of humanity, Taylor Stone thinks there's nothing left to live for, until she meets Kate, a woman who makes her realize love is still alive and makes her dream of a future she thought was no longer possible. (978-1-60282-234-4)

Accidents Never Happen by David-Matthew Barnes. From the moment Albert and Joey meet by chance beneath a train track on a street in Chicago, a domino effect is triggered, setting off a chain reaction of murder and tragedy. (978-1-60282-235-1)

In Plain View by Shane Allison. Best-selling gay erotica authors create the stories of sex and desire modern readers crave. (978-1-60282-236-8)

Wild by Meghan O'Brien. Shapeshifter Selene Rhodes dreads the full moon and the loss of control it brings, but when she rescues forensic pathologist Eve Thomas from a vicious attack by a masked man, she discovers she isn't the scariest monster in San Francisco. (978-1-60282-227-6)

Reluctant Hope by Erin Dutton. Cancer survivor Addison Hunt knows she can't offer any guarantees, in love or in life, and after experiencing a loss of her own, Brooke Donahue isn't willing to risk her heart. (978-1-60282-228-3)

Conquest by Ronica Black. When Mary Brunelle stumbles into the arms of Jude Jaeger, a gorgeous dominatrix at a private nightclub, she is smitten, but she soon finds out Jude is her professor, and Professor Jaeger doesn't date her students...or her conquests. (978-1-60282-229-0)

The Affair of the Porcelain Dog by Jess Faraday. What darkness stalks the London streets at night? Ira Adler, present plaything of crime lord Cain Goddard, will soon find out. (978-1-60282-230-6)

365 Days by K.E. Payne. Life sucks when you're seventeen years old and confused about your sexuality, and the girl of your dreams doesn't even know you exist. Then in walks sexy new emo girl, Hannah Harrison. Clemmie Atkins has exactly 365 days to discover herself, and she's going to have a blast doing it! (978-1-60282-540-6)

Darkness Embraced by Winter Pennington. Surrounded by harsh vampire politics and secret ambitions, Epiphany learns that an old enemy is plotting treason against the woman she once loved, and to save all she holds dear, she must embrace and form an alliance with the dark. (978-1-60282-221-4)

78 Keys by Kristin Marra. When the cosmic powers choose Devorah Rosten to be their next gladiator, she must use her unique skills to try to save her lover, herself, and even humankind. (978-1-60282-222-1)

Playing Passion's Game by Lesley Davis. Trent Williams's only passion in life is gaming—until Juliet Sullivan makes her realize that love can be a whole different game to play. (978-1-60282-223-8)

Retirement Plan by Martha Miller. A modern morality tale of justice, retribution, and women who refuse to be politely invisible. (978-1-60282-224-5)

Who Dat Whodunnit by Greg Herren. Popular New Orleans detective Scotty Bradley investigates the murder of a dethroned beauty queen to clear the name of his pro football–playing cousin. (978-1-60282-225-2)

The Company He Keeps by Dale Chase. A riotously erotic collection of stories set in the sexually repressed and therefore sexually rampant Victorian era. (978-1-60282-226-9)

Cursebusters! by Julie Smith. Budding-psychic Reeno is the most accomplished teenage burglar in California, but one tiny screw-up and poof!—she's sentenced to Bad Girl School. And that isn't even her worst problem. Her sister Haley's dying of an illness no one can diagnose, and now she can't even help. (978-1-60282-559-8)

True Confessions by PJ Trebelhorn. Lynn Patrick finally has a chance with the only woman she's ever loved, her lifelong friend Jessica Greenfield, but Jessie is still tormented by an abusive past. (978-1-60282-216-0)

Ghosts of Winter by Rebecca S. Buck. Can Ros Wynne, who has lost everything she thought defined her, find her true life—and her true love—surrounded by the lingering history of the once-grand Winter Manor? (978-1-60282-219-1)